The Smoke Screen Mystery

When Frank and Joe reached the firehouse, Chief Sullivan had already started to address the group of volunteer fire fighters about the practice drill. "Okay, guys," Sullivan said, "the drill starts *now*. Get moving. And remember, I'm timing you!"

Joe, Frank, and the other fire fighters sprang into action, putting on their protective clothing and making sure the hoses, ladders, and fire extinguishers were secure on the trucks. Then they quickly boarded the engines.

Suddenly the red phone in the firehouse rang, and the chief picked up the receiver.

"At least the caller has good timing," Joe cracked, but his expression grew serious when he saw the grim look on Sullivan's face.

"Burning garage!" the chief shouted, slamming down the phone. Then he barked out the address.

Joe looked at Frank in horror and cried, "That's *our* garage! Aunt C   n there. She could be

The Hardy Boys Mystery Stories

Available from MINSTREL Books

105

The HARDY BOYS®

THE SMOKE SCREEN MYSTERY

FRANKLIN W. DIXON

A MINSTREL® BOOK

PUBLISHED BY POCKET BOOKS

New York   London   Toronto   Sydney   Tokyo   Singapore

A MINSTREL PAPERBACK *ORIGINAL*

 A Minstrel Book published by
POCKET BOOKS, a division of Simon & Schuster Inc.
1230 Avenue of the Americas, New York, NY 10020

Copyright © 1990 by Simon & Schuster Inc.
Cover artwork copyright © 1990 by Paul Bachem
Produced by Mega-Books of New York, Inc.

ISBN: 0-671-69284-4

First Minstrel Books printing December 1990

10 9 8 7 6 5 4 3 2

Contents

THE SMOKE
SCREEN MYSTERY

1 A Hot Story

"That was definitely the worst pizza in Bayport," said Joe Hardy. The muscular seventeen-year-old shook his blond head disdainfully as he climbed into the back of the black police van he and his brother owned. "Whose idea was it to try this new pizza place, anyway?" he asked, turning to his dark-haired girlfriend, Iola, sitting beside him.

"Yours, remember?" replied Frank. At six foot one, eighteen-year-old Frank was an inch taller and slightly thinner than his younger brother and had dark hair and brown eyes. He got into the driver's seat as his girlfriend, Callie Shaw, got in

1

on the passenger side. "You said you wanted to spend your winter vacation playing hockey, going to the latest movies, *and* checking out the new burger and pizza places." Frank adjusted his seat belt, then turned the key and flicked on the headlights. He drove the van out of the parking lot of Pizzaworks, a newly opened pizza restaurant on the outskirts of Bayport, their hometown.

"That sounds like a pretty quiet vacation for you two," Callie said. She pushed her blond hair away from her face and looked curiously from Frank to Joe with her soft brown eyes. "I can't believe you guys didn't plan to take a trip somewhere next week."

"I thought about going away," said Iola Morton with a sigh. "This is the perfect time to head south for some sun. If I didn't have to work during vacation, I'd definitely take off for Florida." Iola worked as a part-time receptionist and secretary for a local real-estate developer.

"The fire chief asked us to stick around," said Joe. "Some of his fire fighters just moved out of Bayport, so he needs all the new volunteers he can get. Frank and I are on call."

"A quiet vacation in Bayport sounds good to me right now," said Frank. "After fighting those two warehouse fires last week, I'm ready for some R and R."

He and Joe had recently finished a sixteen-week course at a state school so that they could become volunteer fire fighters for the Bayport Fire Department. Their work with the fire department had been fairly tame at first. They had helped to put out some small fires, rescued a cat from a tree, and responded to two false alarms. But in the past week they'd learned just how grueling fire fighting could be. Twice recently they had spent the better part of a night battling warehouse fires. They had been the most exhausting hours Frank and Joe had ever experienced, and now they were looking forward to a week of taking it easy.

"That fire yesterday totally destroyed our Friday night plans," Joe said. "I mean, we could have—"

"Had the worst pizza in Bayport *last* night instead of tonight," Callie finished with a grin.

Iola laughed so that her short hair bounced around her ears. But then a serious look came into her eyes. "You're not the only one whose plans were ruined by last night's fire," she told Joe. "I was at work this morning when Donald Pierce—that's my boss—found out about it. He owns that warehouse *and* the first one that burned down. He's pretty upset."

Light flecks of snow began to fall, illuminated by the van's headlights. Frank flicked on the windshield wipers and said, "Well, at least no

3

one was hurt. And Pierce will probably get the money from his insurance claim pretty quickly," he said. "I heard the new fire inspector say that the fires were definitely caused by faulty wiring, so the insurance procedures are fairly simple. If an arsonist had torched the warehouses, the claim could be held up for a long time by an investigation."

"You know, we haven't investigated an arson case in quite a while," Joe said. "What if these warehouse fires . . ."

"Weren't accidental?" Frank said, finishing his brother's sentence. "That's not what the inspector said." Frank turned off the highway onto a curving exit ramp. There were patches of ice on the ramp, and Frank drove slowly and carefully to avoid skidding.

"Okay, okay," said Joe. "I guess I was just looking for a little detective action to spice up our quiet vacation."

Callie turned in the front seat to look back at Joe. "If you want some spice, you should read the special series on Bayport real estate that's been running in the *Bayport Examiner* for the past few weeks," she said.

Frank chuckled. "My brother read the newspaper? You've got to be kidding!"

"Hey, I read a lot of newspapers," Joe said indignantly.

4

"Yeah, right," Frank said, rolling his eyes. "The sports pages and the comics."

"Well, the *Examiner* series is really incredible," Callie continued, ignoring the Hardys' banter. "You wouldn't believe how many truly terrible landlords and shady real-estate developers there are in Bayport. And guess who's at the top of the list?"

"Donald Pierce," Iola responded. "I've been reading the series, too. That's another reason Pierce hasn't been too happy lately. The series has been portraying him as the worst landlord in Bayport. The *Examiner* said today that he is responsible for the warehouse fires because he was too cheap to have the wiring checked."

"The real-estate series was Sam Dawson's idea," Callie said. "He's the new owner of the *Examiner*." Callie sometimes worked part-time as a stringer for the *Examiner*, so she heard some of the office gossip. "The paper was losing money before he bought it," she continued, "but now circulation is way up."

Frank was just pulling up in front of Callie's house when the beeper on the van's dashboard began to sound.

"Another fire. I can't believe it," Joe said with a groan as his brother stopped the van.

"Believe it," Frank said grimly. "The beeper's our signal that there's a fire in progress some-

5

where in Bayport," he explained to Callie and Iola. Switching off the beeper, he reached for the van's phone. He pressed the autodial and was instantly connected with the firehouse. After listening for a few moments, he said, "Right, we're on our way," then hung up.

"Where's the fire?" asked Joe.

"It's a two-family house at Thirty-seven Broad Street, just off Main," answered Frank.

Callie and Iola had unfastened their seat belts and started to climb out of the van, looking at each other anxiously. Suddenly they stopped short, "Oh, no!" Iola cried with a gasp.

"That's Jen's house!" exclaimed Callie. She turned to Frank and Joe. "You guys know Jen Buckley. She's a good friend of ours."

Frank nodded. "In that case, you two had better come with us," he said. "She might need your help. Let's go!"

The girls scrambled back into their seats. They barely had time to refasten their seat belts before Frank turned the van around with a screech of tires and headed toward downtown Bayport. As they raced down Main Street, he saw a fire engine and a hook and ladder truck ahead of the van and heard the whine of their sirens.

About a half mile down Main Street, Frank turned left onto Broad Street and immediately spotted the burning building. The thick smoke engulfing the structure made it almost indistinguishable. Seeing the fire chief's red car, Frank pulled up behind it, and he and Joe jumped out of the van.

A shiny new sports car zoomed up a second later, stopping behind the van. Frank looked over his shoulder and saw that the newly arrived fire fighter was Scott Malone. Tall, dark-haired, and in his early twenties, Scott caught up with Frank and Joe as they hurried over to one of the fire engines.

"I can't believe Kevin's not here yet," Scott said, glancing around as he and the Hardys began to pull on their protective pants, coats, boots, gloves, and hats. "This is the third fire he's been late responding to."

Joe nodded. Kevin Thomas, another volunteer fire fighter, was Scott's best friend. Joe and Frank had known Kevin for several years.

"I'm kind of worried about Kevin," continued Scott. "I mean, don't you guys think he's been acting a little strange ever since he was fired from his superintendent's job last week?"

Joe shrugged absently. He had noticed Kevin's lateness, and it was pretty obvious that he was upset about being fired from his full-time job. But the blazing fire was the first thing on Joe's mind right now. Although he couldn't actually go into a burning building because he wasn't yet eighteen,

Joe was anxious to get into action manning the hose. Joe ran over to the fire trucks and began helping other fire fighters roll out the hose that was attached to the truck.

"We can talk about Kevin later," said Frank. "Let's go!" He handed an air pack to Scott and grabbed one for himself.

"Hardy, Malone!" Frank heard the fire chief, Tom Sullivan, bark. "Help Collins and Ravitch get people out of the house. Move it!"

Frank and Scott strapped the air pack canisters onto their backs and rushed toward the house. Flames were shooting out of the first-floor windows on each side of the house, and thick smoke rose into the air.

Frank raced up the porch steps, Scott right behind him. Two fire fighters were escorting an elderly couple out the door of the apartment on the left, so Frank ran toward the door on the right, which was still closed. It burst open just as he reached it, and out staggered Jen Buckley and her mother, their faces streaked with sweat and dirt.

"Help . . . my . . ." Mrs. Buckley began, but she was gasping and coughing too violently to speak. Jen was coughing, too. Frank and Scott helped them down the steps and away from the smoke. A fire fighter rushed over with an air tank

8

and fitted masks over Jen's and her mother's frightened faces.

"My little brother, Matt!" Jen rasped after taking a few breaths. She looked at Frank, her eyes wide with fear. "He's still in there! You've got to get him—" Then she began to cough again.

"Where is he?" asked Frank.

Jen pointed to a window on the second floor. "He pulled away from me when we got to the door," she said breathlessly.

Frank turned to the fire fighter who was manning the ladder truck. "I need a ladder placed at that window!" he shouted, pointing.

Frank grabbed a pry bar and a hatchet, then hurried back toward the house. Joe and the others were dousing the flames on the left side of the house, but the right side was blazing more than ever, and smoke poured out of all the second-floor windows.

Frank rushed up the porch steps and ran to the Buckleys' door. Through the open door, he could see that, although the stairs were still clear, flames had covered the outside wall and were creeping up to the ceiling. Adjusting the air pack's mask over his face, Frank took a deep breath and plunged into the burning house.

2 Deadly Flames

Frank climbed the stairs two at a time. The heat was intense, but he knew his protective clothing would keep him fairly cool.

There was dense smoke on the upstairs landing, but at least all the flames Frank had seen on the lower level hadn't yet reached the second floor. He stopped and listened. It was hard to hear anything over the roar of the fire, but he thought he could hear a child crying in a room to his left. He raced over to the closed door and rattled the knob, but the door was locked.

"Stand back from the door!" Frank called to the boy inside. Frank raised his ax and began to chop the wooden door. A few moments later he had hacked a ragged opening in the door. He dropped the ax and reached in to pop the lock open. Then he stepped quickly into the room. It was just beginning to fill up with smoke.

Through the haze, Frank could see a little boy sitting on the floor. He looked to be about five years old, and he was tightly clutching a teddy bear. His eyes widened when he saw Frank. "Are you a fireman?" Matt asked.

Frank nodded and gave the little boy a reassuring smile as he knelt down and fitted his air mask over Matt's nose and mouth.

"We're going to crawl to the window," Frank explained. "Then I want you to climb up on me and put your arms around my neck. Okay, buddy?"

Matt nodded.

When they got to the window, Frank raised it and looked out. He was relieved to see the top of the rescue ladder leaning against the wall under the window. Kevin Thomas was on the ground, holding the ladder steady with his gloved hands.

Frank turned to Matt. "We'll throw your bear down to Kevin, okay?" he said. The little boy handed him the teddy bear, and Frank threw it down. Then Frank knelt on the window ledge, turned, and stepped onto the first rung of the ladder. He reached for Matt and said, "Now, hold on tight," as the boy wrapped his legs around

Frank's middle and his arms around his shoulders. Frank climbed carefully down the ladder.

When he reached the ground, Frank handed Matt over to Kevin. Letting out a sigh of relief, Frank watched as Kevin carried the little boy to an emergency medical truck to be examined by a paramedic. Then Frank walked over to the fire engine and sat on the step below the driver's door. His eyes were burning, and his chest was aching from the smoke. Setting his air canister on the ground in front of him, he held the mask to his face and inhaled.

"Much better," he murmured after taking a few breaths. He closed his eyes for a moment, and when he opened them, he saw Kevin walking toward him. The red-haired, muscular young man was a few inches taller than Frank.

"Is Matt okay?" Frank asked anxiously.

Kevin nodded. "He's fine. He's with his mother and sister now. And Joe and the rest of the crew just finished putting out the fire."

Frank glanced over and saw his brother bending over the hydrant and turning off the water. Scott and a few other fire fighters, armed with fire extinguishers, were entering the house to douse any flames that remained. The fire inspector was heading for the house, too.

A moment later Joe joined Frank and Kevin. "My brother, the hero," Joe said with a grin.

Then he glanced down. "Uh, Frank, did you happen to notice that there's a stuffed animal sitting on your lap?"

Frank looked down at his lap and laughed. "It's Matt's teddy bear," he explained.

Kevin laughed and said, "I thought you might be missing it."

"I'd better give it back to Matt." Frank stood up but lingered by the engine for a moment. Turning to Kevin, he said, "Look, I know it's none of my business, but why were you late again? I mean, I know how serious you are about fire fighting, and it's kind of surprising that you—"

"You're right, Frank," Kevin interrupted. "It *is* none of your business." He turned and walked away toward the ladder truck.

Joe gave a low whistle. "What's his problem, anyway?" he said, gesturing toward Kevin with his thumb.

"He's a pretty private person," said Frank with a shrug.

Frank and Joe walked over to where Jen, her mother, and Matt were standing with Callie and Iola. Frank handed Matt his teddy bear, and the little boy gazed up at him admiringly.

"I can't thank you enough for rescuing my son," Mrs. Buckley said, smiling at Frank. She turned to Joe. "And thank you for putting the fire

13

out so quickly." Her smile faded, however, as her gaze went to the dripping, soot-blackened house.

Jen put her arm around her mother's shoulders. "We'll be okay, Mom. The landlord will get the house rebuilt. And in the meantime, Callie said we can stay with her. Her father is coming to pick us up."

Callie nudged Frank. "See that guy over there?" She pointed to a short, wiry, sandy-haired young man standing with Chief Sullivan and the fire inspector. "That's Mark Maguire, the new reporter for the *Examiner.* He's the guy who's been writing the real-estate series."

Just then the fire chief walked up to Frank, Joe, and the others, followed closely by Maguire. Chief Sullivan, a burly, middle-aged man with a thick brown head of hair and beard, cleared his throat. "Mrs. Buckley," he said gruffly, "the fire inspector has just informed me that the fire was caused by faulty wiring. Your landlord will have to have the building rewired before it's renovated."

"Donald Pierce is the owner and landlord," Mrs. Buckley told the fire chief in an angry voice. "I can't believe this. He should have had the wiring checked in such an old house."

"Pierce again," Joe said quietly to Iola. "Your boss is definitely *not* the luckiest landlord in Bayport right now."

14

Iola nodded. "Pierce is going to hit the roof when he hears about this third fire."

Frank watched Maguire busily jot down notes on a pad as Chief Sullivan and Mrs. Buckley talked. Frank noticed that when Donald Pierce's name was mentioned, Maguire jerked up his head, then smiled a little and nodded before he began writing again. And when the fire chief left after making sure the Buckleys had a place to stay, Mark Maguire remained behind.

"I'd appreciate a statement from you about Donald Pierce," Maguire said to Mrs. Buckley after introducing himself. "Would you say he was a good landlord?"

"After this fire? Absolutely not!" Mrs. Buckley replied angrily. "I'd say he was a *terrible* landlord. He's responsible for this fire, and I want him and everyone else in this town to know it!"

"Great statement, Mrs. Buckley. Thanks," Maguire said, smiling broadly. "Well, got to get the presses rolling. Sorry about the fire." He turned and jogged off.

A moment later Callie's father pulled up to the curb in the Shaws' station wagon. Jen, Matt, and Mrs. Buckley wearily followed Callie and Iola over to the car. Frank saw that the elderly couple who lived in the apartment next to the Buckleys were being helped into a car behind the Shaws.

"I wonder if Maguire got a statement from

them, too," Joe said, gesturing to the couple as he and Frank headed toward the fire truck.

Frank picked up an air pack and checked the air gauge. "I'm sure you'll be able to read all about it in tomorrow's *Examiner*," he replied, placing the pack in the truck. "If you can tear yourself away from the hockey scores, that is."

"Did I hear someone mention hockey?" said a voice behind them. Frank turned and saw Scott smiling at them. He had taken off his fire-fighting clothes and was putting on a leather jacket. "We're still playing hockey tomorrow morning, right? You two, me, and Kevin?"

"Right," said Joe. He sat on the engine steps and began to pull off his boots. "But not too early, okay? These blue eyes need lots of rest so they can focus on winging that puck past you and into the goal net!"

"Yeah, well, we'll see who wings who," Scott said with a laugh. "Kevin and I will pick you up at eleven." He turned to Kevin, who was walking toward them carrying two fire extinguishers. "Eleven o'clock okay with you, buddy?" asked Scott.

"Right, hockey tomorrow," Kevin said. "Yeah, sure, eleven's fine." Falling silent, he began hoisting the canisters up into the truck.

Frank was looking curiously at Kevin, thinking that his friend seemed preoccupied, when he

16

heard Chief Sullivan call out, "Okay, you guys, let's finish packing up so we can get back to the firehouse. Then you can all get a well-deserved good night's sleep!"

Frank, Joe, Kevin, and Scott sprang into action. Twenty minutes later all the equipment was back in place on the fire engines. Soon after that, Joe and Frank were back in their van and heading home.

When Joe walked into the kitchen the next morning, Frank was eating French toast and reading the Sunday *Examiner*.

"It's on the front page," Frank told him.

Joe sat down at the table and reached for a glass of orange juice. "What is?" he asked. "The fire and how the heroic Hardys saved the day? The night, I mean."

"The fire is featured," Frank said, looking at him over the top of the paper. "And so is Donald Pierce. Listen to this headline: 'Homeless, Angry Tenants Blame Loser Landlord.'"

Joe laughed. "That should grab the readers' attention. What does the article say?"

Frank read silently, then looked up, a puzzled expression on his face. "You know, it's weird. Maguire used only one short paragraph to describe the fire. The rest of the article talks about Pierce and what a crooked character he is."

17

Joe looked up as their aunt Gertrude walked into the kitchen. "I've just been on the phone with your mother," the heavy-set, middle-aged woman told Frank and Joe. She went to the refrigerator and took out three eggs. "She's having a good time at her cousin's. Naturally, I told her how worried I was about you boys and your fire-fighting work, but . . ." She let her voice trail off and shook her head as she began to prepare another batch of French toast.

Joe looked at his brother and rolled his eyes. Over the years, Joe and Frank had learned to live with their aunt Gertrude's motherly worrying.

Joe got up, stepped over to the counter, and gave his aunt a kiss on the cheek. "But Mom told you that we could take care of ourselves, right?"

"Well, yes, but—" Aunt Gertrude began.

"Did she say how Dad's case in Washington is coming, Aunt Gert?" Frank asked quickly. Fenton Hardy, Frank and Joe's father, was a retired New York City police officer who had become a private detective.

Before Aunt Gertrude could reply, the front doorbell rang.

"If that's Kevin and Scott, they're a little early," Frank commented, glancing at his watch. He got up and headed for the front door.

When he opened the door, Frank was surprised to see a stocky, well-dressed man of medium height standing on the doorstep. He looked to be in his early forties, and he was holding a copy of the *Examiner*.

"I take it you're one of the Hardy brothers," the man said, looking Frank over. "I'd like to speak with the two of you. My name is Donald Pierce."

Frank blinked in surprise. What could Bayport's most infamous landlord want with him and Joe? "Come in," Frank said, opening the door wider. Donald Pierce stepped into the living room and began to unbutton his overcoat.

"I'm Frank Hardy," said Frank. "My brother, Joe, is in the kitchen. I'll get him."

"You're not going to believe who's here," Frank said to Joe in a low voice as he entered the kitchen. "Donald Pierce!"

Joe raised his eyebrows. "Well, what do you know," he said. "Maybe he wants to tear down our house and build a skyscraper here instead." Joe hastily finished the last of his French toast and followed his brother.

When the Hardys had walked into the living room, Donald Pierce was standing next to the sofa. "I'm a busy man, so if you don't mind, I'll get right to the point," Pierce said briskly. "I've heard that you two are successful detectives, and I want you to investigate something for me." He looked from Frank to Joe. "Can you do it?"

19

"That depends on what it is," Frank said warily.

Pierce nodded and sat down on the sofa. He tapped the newspaper he was carrying. "Have you read the article on last night's fire in today's *Examiner?*" he asked.

"I read it," Frank said. "In fact, my brother and I were there. We're volunteer fire fighters."

"Three fires caused by faulty wiring is unbelievably bad luck, Mr. Pierce," added Joe.

Pierce leaned forward. "Well, that's just it. It *is* unbelievable, because it's not true. I don't think the fires were accidents. I think they were arson."

"But the fire inspector said the fires were accidental," Frank said.

"He's new on the job, right?" Pierce asked. The Hardys nodded. "And arsonists can be very clever at hiding evidence." He paused for a moment, then said, "I already have a very strong suspect. A man named Kevin Thomas."

"What!" Joe exclaimed. "That's crazy! Kevin is a fire fighter, and not only that, he's our friend. He couldn't be an arsonist!"

"Relax, Joe," Frank said quietly. He turned to Pierce. "Why do you suspect Kevin?"

"Motive," Pierce replied promptly. "Until recently, he worked as a superintendent in one of my apartment buildings. I had to fire him, for incompetence and because he had an uncontrollable temper. After I let him go, he swore he'd get me for firing him. It's revenge, pure and simple."

Frank turned toward one of the living room windows, where he thought he saw something move. He stepped over to the window, opened it a little, and looked outside, but didn't see anything. "If you're so convinced the fires were arson," Frank said, turning back to Donald, "why don't you go to the police with your suspicions?"

Pierce dismissed the idea with a wave of his hand. "A waste of time," he said. "The police are satisfied the fires were accidents. No, I need to have this investigated privately." He held out the newspaper. "Listen, the bad press I've been getting in the *Examiner* is starting to affect my real-estate projects. After last night's fire, I'm going to have a hard time convincing banks, contractors, and potential tenants to do business with me."

"And you think proving the fires were arson will clear your reputation," Frank said.

"And get the *Examiner* off your back," added Joe.

"That's right," Pierce said, nodding. "I think Sam Dawson and his hotshot reporter Mark Maguire are trying to sell papers by trashing powerful people like me. Why Dawson is picking on me, and where he's getting his dirt from, I don't know, but it's got to be stopped!'' He stood up and looked at Frank and Joe purposefully. "So I repeat my question: Will you take the case?"

"Well, before we take this case," Joe said, "you should understand that I think you're way out of line about Kevin, and—" Before he could finish his sentence, the doorbell rang.

Frank opened the door, and Scott and Kevin stepped into the house. "So, are you guys ready for the hockey match of the century?" Scott asked with a grin. Then he spotted Pierce. "Hey, I'm sorry. I didn't realize you had company."

Kevin had been smiling, but his smile faded when he saw Donald Pierce. His face turned red with rage, and he shouted, "Pierce, you creep! I'll get you!"

With that, Kevin raised his fists and lunged at the real-estate developer.

3 Friend or Foe?

"Kevin, wait!" Joe rushed forward to restrain his friend, and Joe's jaw took the full force of Kevin's fist. Reeling backward, Joe fell against the door of the hall closet and stood there stunned, his eyes blank.

"Joe! Are you okay?" Frank asked.

Joe gave his head a shake and blinked. Then he felt his jaw tenderly. "Yeah, I'm fine," he said. He looked past Frank to where Kevin and Scott stood. "Whew, that was some wallop!"

Kevin had a stunned expression on his face. "I'm sorry, Joe," he said at last. "That was a really dumb thing to do. I . . . I guess I just have to learn to control my temper."

23

"No hard feelings," said Joe, wincing as he massaged his aching jaw. "You could work a little harder at it, though."

Joe noticed that Pierce was standing at the far end of the living room—as far away from Kevin, it seemed, as he could get. Joe wondered if Kevin was going to apologize to Pierce, but Kevin didn't even look in the real-estate developer's direction.

Pierce turned to Frank and said in an icy tone, "I'll call you later to find out if you'll take the case, but here's my card if you want to reach me." He handed the slip of paper to Frank, then said, "After what just took place here, I'm confident that you will." He brushed by Kevin and Scott and left the house.

"Hey, I just realized who that guy is," Scott said, jerking his thumb at the door. "That's Donald Pierce, Bayport's 'Loser Landlord.' What was he doing here?"

"That's what I'd like to know," Kevin said, shooting a searching look at Frank and Joe. "What did he mean when he said he was confident you'd take the case?"

Instead of answering Kevin's questions, Frank asked quietly, "Why did Donald Pierce fire you, Kevin?"

Kevin's face began to turn red again. "That greedy creep fired me because I had a broken elevator fixed in the apartment building where I was the super," he said hotly. "I was just doing my job!"

"But why would he fire you for fixing something?" Joe asked in a puzzled tone.

Kevin turned to Joe. "Don't you see? Pierce ordered me not to have the elevator fixed because he didn't want to spend the money. But I had it fixed anyway. When he saw the bill, Pierce blew his top and fired me. That's the kind of guy you're working for!"

"Why are you working for him, anyway?" Scott asked.

"Hey, we haven't agreed to take the case," Joe told the two boys. "Pierce came to us because he thinks the fire last night and the two warehouse fires last week were cases of arson," explained Joe.

"Arson!" exclaimed Scott and Kevin at the same time.

"That's crazy!" Scott added. "The fire inspector said they were caused by faulty wiring!"

Joe shrugged. "Well, Pierce doesn't agree. He thinks that because the fire inspector is new on the job, he missed the evidence of arson."

Frank looked at Kevin. Taking a deep breath, he said, "Kevin, we need to know exactly what you meant when you said you'd 'get' Pierce for firing you."

Kevin stared at Frank, and his mouth fell open.

"Are you saying that Pierce thinks *I* set those fires to get revenge?" he asked in disbelief. "What about you guys? Do you think I'm an arsonist, too?"

"No way." Joe shook his head firmly. "We think Pierce is way off base, right, Frank?" He turned to his brother.

Joe, Scott, and Kevin were all looking at Frank expectantly, but Frank just stood there silently. It would be premature to accuse Kevin without any proof, but Frank had to admit that Kevin had a motive.

Kevin must have sensed Frank's thoughts. The muscular, red-haired young man glared at Frank, then turned and slammed out of the house.

After an awkward silence, Scott said, "I think we should reschedule our hockey game for tomorrow morning. Okay, guys? Right now I'd better go try to calm Kevin down. Losing that job was really rough on him. And now this . . ." He shook his head and hurried out the door.

"Why didn't you stick up for Kevin?" Joe demanded as soon as the door closed. "He's our friend. I can't believe you suspect him of being an arsonist!"

Frank was putting his hockey stick back in the hall closet. He turned to face his brother. "If Pierce is right and the fires were set on purpose, that means there's an arsonist on the loose. I want to believe Kevin's innocent, but right now he's got to be a prime suspect. He's a fire fighter, so he knows how fires are set. Plus, he's got a motive—revenge. And he was late for all three fires, so he could have set them and then shown up later to help fight them."

Frank walked back to the living room as he talked. Joe lay down on the couch and put an arm behind his head.

"Well, if you ask me, Pierce is just a lousy landlord who's trying to get off the hook," Joe said.

"Could be," admitted Frank, sitting down in the easy chair opposite the couch. "But I think we do need to take this case, for two reasons—"

"To prove that Kevin is innocent," Joe broke in quickly.

"Right," agreed Frank. "And to stop the arsonist from striking again. But first," he added, "we have to find out if the fires really were arson."

"Should we start at Jen's house or one of the warehouses?"

"Let's see. The Buckleys and their neighbors will be at the house today sifting through their personal belongings," Frank said. "So let's try the first warehouse that burned."

Aunt Gertrude bustled into the living room

carrying a dust rag. She shook her head disapprovingly when she saw a window open. "It's winter no matter what the thermometer says," she muttered, hurrying past Joe to the window. "Even though it's warm today, you boys can still catch your deaths of—"

Suddenly she dropped her dust rag and let out a scream.

Joe sprang up from the sofa. "Aunt Gert, what's wrong?"

"There's a man in our bushes!" she shrieked.

Joe rushed over to the window. He immediately recognized the short, wiry man. It was Mark Maguire, the reporter from the *Examiner*, and he was running down the block to his car.

Frowning, Joe put his arm around his shaking aunt. "It's okay, Aunt Gert," he said soothingly. "That was just a newspaper reporter we saw last night at the fire, not a burglar."

"Poor Aunt Gert," Frank said, chuckling. "I guess you'll never get used to us being detectives *or* fire fighters."

"You're probably right, Frank. I never will." Aunt Gertrude, calmer now, picked up her dust rag and headed up the stairs.

"How much do you think Maguire overheard?" asked Joe.

Frank shrugged. "Maybe everything. I thought

I heard something outside the window before Kevin and Scott showed up. Maguire must have followed Pierce here. The question is, will he print the information he got?"

"If he does, it could jeopardize our whole investigation," said Joe. "The arsonist—if there is one—could make a special effort to cover his tracks."

"Then we should get moving. We'll check out the warehouses, then hit Jen's house later," Frank said. "After all, if we don't find evidence of arson, this case will be closed anyway."

"I remember the way to that first warehouse. Let's go!" Joe grabbed his jacket and headed out the door to their van, ahead of his brother.

Half an hour later Joe turned the van down Enterprise Way, the main road of an industrial park on the outskirts of Bayport.

"Here we are." Joe braked to a halt and looked up at the soot-blackened warehouse that sat on a hill at the end of the road. A charred sign on the large, wooden building read "Datco Business Machines."

Joe put his foot back on the gas pedal and drove up the long driveway that led to the warehouse. The paved surface was thick with slush, and he had to drive very slowly to keep the van from slipping.

"Let's start inside," Frank said as he and Joe got out of the van.

Joe followed his brother to the double metal doors, which were unlocked.

The Hardys stepped into the warehouse, and Joe paused to look around. The huge, high-ceilinged space was empty, he saw, except for a few metal filing cabinets and desks.

"I remember being told that fire burns up and out," Joe said, as he and Frank began to wander around the warehouse. "So a V-shaped pattern in the scorch marks will tell us where the fire originated." He looked over his shoulder and saw his brother crouch down under the only unbroken window in the building. The window was almost completely covered with soot. "What are you doing?" Joe asked, coming to stand a few feet away from Frank.

"Checking the wiring that's jutting out from the wall down here. It's charred and definitely old and frayed." Frank leaned his head back and stared at the wall above the socket. "Look, there's a big V-pattern here, too, so this must be where the fire started. It looks like this fire really was an accident." He stood up.

Joe started to move closer to Frank to get a better look at the wiring. Suddenly a crashing noise of breaking glass erupted over Frank's head, and Joe looked up in surprise. Shards of glass were showering down around his brother, and a fire extinguisher was flying through the window straight at Frank!

4 Special Delivery

"Watch out!" shouted Joe. He hurled himself at his brother, pushing Frank onto the floor away from the fire extinguisher. A split second later it crashed to the floor right where Frank had been.

"What the . . . ?" Frank gasped. Joe's tackle had knocked some of the wind out of him, but after taking a few deep breaths, he was able to breathe normally. "What was that?" he asked, sitting up slowly.

"It's a fire extinguisher with a note attached," Joe said. Joe stopped short as the sound of a car door slamming filtered into the warehouse, followed by the roar of an engine being started.

Frank quickly jumped up and headed for the

door. "Forget that for now!" he shouted over his shoulder to Joe. "Let's try to catch up to the guy!"

Joe scrambled to his feet, picked up the canister, and followed Frank out of the warehouse in time to see a blue van backing slowly down the slippery warehouse driveway. Frank heard Joe's footsteps behind him as he raced around the side of the building to their black van and got in. Joe hopped in as Frank started the engine.

The tires squealed as Frank backed up and quickly turned the van in the direction of the driveway. The blue van had turned onto Enterprise Way, Frank saw, and was beginning to pick up speed. Frank pressed down on the accelerator.

"Take it easy!" Joe exclaimed, gripping the dashboard as the van went into a skid.

"I'm doing the best I can," Frank said between clenched teeth as he steadied the van. "Hold on!"

Frank swerved onto Enterprise Way and gunned the engine. By now the blue van was about half a mile ahead of them, approaching the end of the road. As the Hardys barreled down the road after the van, it made a right turn and disappeared.

"We're losing it," Joe said.

Just then they heard the clanging of a railroad

crossing signal and the whistle of an approaching train. Frank glanced at his brother and grinned. "That crossing is a few yards down the road he just turned onto," he said. "Our friend will *have* to stop for the train."

They were almost to the end of Enterprise Way when they saw the blue van zoom past them on the cross street.

Frank turned the van in a sharp, screeching left turn and began to follow the other van down the deserted road. "Did you get a look at the driver?" he asked.

"No," answered Joe. "The window was tinted. Try to move closer so we can get the license plate number."

Frank pressed down hard on the gas pedal, and their van shot forward. Soon they were only a few yards behind the other van.

"The license plate is smudged, totally unreadable," Joe reported in a voice tinged with frustration. "The only other identifying feature is a broken tailpipe. Wait, he's slowing down a little," he added. "Maybe we can force him off the road into a snowbank."

Ahead, Frank could see two entrance ramps that led to the highway. With a burst of speed, the blue van zoomed under a bridge and swerved onto the ramp on the left.

Frank followed the van onto the highway. He

managed to stay fairly close, even though there was a steady stream of traffic.

Without warning, the blue van swerved into the passing lane in front of a huge tractor-trailer. At the same time another tractor-trailer came barreling up the next entrance ramp at top speed, and Frank had to slow down to let it onto the highway. He let out a groan. Now the two tractor-trailers were traveling side by side in front of him and the blue van had disappeared from view.

"If I could just get around this guy . . ." muttered Frank. He peered into the sideview mirror to check the traffic in the left lane.

Finally there was an opening, and Frank maneuvered the Hardys' van into the passing lane and ahead of the truck in the cruising lane. But there was no sign of the blue van.

"I don't believe this," Joe blurted out. "He must have gotten off the highway in front of that truck. That was the only exit we passed."

"I guess you're right," Frank said, shaking his head. "Why don't you read me the note that's taped to the fire extinguisher?" Frank drove into the right-hand lane and headed down the next exit ramp.

Joe reached down, pulled the folded paper off the metal canister, and read aloud: " 'Stop investigating for Pierce now—*or else*. This is your first warning. Let's hope it's the last.' "

As Joe read, Frank turned the van and drove to the entrance ramp that would get them back on the highway going in the opposite direction.

"Whoever wrote the note and tossed the fire extinguisher through the window knew—or guessed—that we were going to the first warehouse that burned," Joe said. Then his blue eyes lit up. "Maguire!" he exclaimed. "He was listening to our conversation. He must have heard us say where we were going!"

Frank nodded. "Right. And then there's Kevin. He could have guessed we'd head for that warehouse." Glancing sideways, Frank saw that his brother was shaking his head stubbornly. "Look, Joe, we have to check out all the suspects, even if they're friends. You know that as well as I do."

They rode on in silence for a few moments before Joe sighed and said, "I hate to admit it, but you're right about Kevin. We have to take him seriously as a suspect. But I can't see how Maguire would figure into an arson picture. What's his motive?"

"We definitely have to find out more about him," replied Frank. "And we still need to come up with some positive proof that the fires were, in fact, arson. That warning note isn't really enough to go on."

"Then let's head back to the warehouse and finish searching for clues," suggested Joe.

By the time the Hardys returned to the Datco warehouse, the sun was starting to sink in the gray winter sky.

"No sign of our friend in the blue van," commented Frank as he pulled into the parking lot behind the building.

He and Joe reentered the warehouse and glanced around. "We'd better work fast," Frank said. "There isn't much light in here now."

Leaving Joe to look for anything unusual, Frank walked over to the window through which their attacker had thrown the canister. Leaning in close to the wall, he studied the wires again. Then he stepped back a couple of feet and looked at the fire-blackened V-shape on the wall.

"There are worn and frayed wires all over this building, and I found another V pattern," said Joe, walking along the edge of the interior to check for more wires. He moved a metal cabinet from the wall and saw something that made him stoop to look closer. It was an empty coffee can, and inside were pieces of torn fabric that hadn't been burned by the fire. The colors and patterns of the material were still visible, and Joe noticed the stench of gasoline as he picked up a piece of plaid flannel. "Look at this!" Joe cried out to his brother, putting the plaid piece in his jacket pocket.

Frank came over and inspected the can, then

37

looked at his brother and said, "Maybe that new inspector *is* inexperienced. Let's keep looking."

Joe and Frank headed for opposite walls, intent on moving any object that could be hiding more evidence.

After twenty minutes, the light became too dim for them to continue. Frank walked over to where his brother had left the coffee can, and Joe came up behind his brother. There was a creaking noise as Joe stepped on one of the floorboards.

Frank whirled around. "Do that again," he urged. "Press down on that board."

Giving his brother a curious look, Joe shifted his weight onto the floorboard, and it creaked again, loudly. "It's a loose board," said Joe. "So what?" Then, realizing what Frank was getting at, he dropped to his knees and began to pull at the loose board with his hands.

"I can't get enough of a handhold," he said after a minute. "We need a pry bar."

"There's one in the van," Frank told him, starting for the door.

A moment later, Frank returned with the pry bar and knelt down beside his brother. He began to wedge a two-foot-long board loose with the tool, and before long the wood came loose with a loud, splintering pop.

"Looks like we picked the right board to pull

up," Joe said excitedly as he and Frank stared into the space below the floor.

Sitting on a small mound of hard-packed dirt was another empty coffee can. A line of charred rags stretched from the can toward the wall by the window.

Frank reached down and pulled out the can. Inside it there was charred fabric. He sniffed at the can, then looked at Joe. "Definitely gasoline," he said. "Our arsonist filled the can with gasoline and lit it. That line of rags carried the fire over to the wall so that it looked as if faulty wiring had started it."

Joe nodded. "The arsonist probably did the same thing under the floor by the wall where I saw the second V pattern."

"I think we should still look for clues at the second warehouse and Jen's house," said Frank. "We might find something that will help us identify the arsonist."

"Good idea," Joe agreed. He peered into the deepening shadows of the warehouse. "But we better put it off until tomorrow. It's already getting too dark to see much. Right now *I* think getting something to eat is our first priority. And I just happened to spot a new pizza place right near the highway. It's called Pizza Your Way."

"Sounds like your kind of place," Frank said

with a smile. He picked up the pry bar and coffee can Joe had found with the fabric that hadn't been burned. He and Joe headed for the warehouse door.

"The pizza's on me," Frank said, "to thank you for keeping me from getting decked by that fire extinguisher!"

Frank and Joe were on their way out the door with their hockey sticks and skates the next morning when they heard Aunt Gertrude call to them. Joe turned and saw his aunt standing in the kitchen doorway.

"I hope you two will be back by this afternoon," she said. "That garage needs to be cleaned out."

"Give us a break, Aunt Gertrude," said Joe. "We're on vacation!"

"I'll start picking up in there, but I'll need you to move some heavy things."

Joe just groaned, but Frank elbowed him in the ribs and promised, "We'll get back here as soon as we can, Aunt Gert. We have a drill at the firehouse this afternoon, but I don't think it will take too long."

Joe looked at his brother and rolled his eyes. "Come on," he whispered. "Let's get out of here before she decides she wants to start on that garage *now!*"

They hurried outside to the van and put their hockey sticks and skates in the back. As Joe pointed the van in the direction of Young's Pond, he and Frank began to discuss the arson case.

"I think we ought to bring Con Riley in on this case," Frank said. Lieutenant Con Riley of the Bayport Police had been a friend of the Hardys for many years. "The police need to be informed that the fire was arson. And we'd better tell the fire chief, too." He thought for a moment, then picked up the van's phone and dialed a number.

"Who are you calling now?" asked Joe. "Con?"

Frank shook his head. "Callie, to ask her to see if she can get work as a stringer again for the *Bayport Examiner*. That way she can keep an eye on Mark Maguire for us. Maybe she can find out something about his background, too." After speaking to Callie for a little while, Frank said, "Great! Keep us posted, okay?" then hung up the phone.

"It's all set," he said to Joe. "Callie's going to call Sam Dawson now."

"Here we are," Joe announced, pulling to a halt at the end of a dead-end road, next to a path that led into the surrounding woods. He pointed to the white sports car parked next to the path. "There's Scott's car. Looks like Kevin's not here yet. Do you want to call Con before we start playing?"

41

Frank shook his head. "Our information will keep for a few hours. Right now I'm ready to get out on the ice."

"Me, too!" Joe took off ahead of his brother down the path that led to the pond. When he emerged from the trees, he spotted Scott sitting on a bench at the pond's edge, lacing up his skates. Scott looked up and grinned when he spotted Joe.

"I'm breaking in new skates and a new stick," he called out as Joe approached the bench. "And I worked late at the supermarket last night, so I might not be so swift on the ice today."

"If you're asking us to go easy on you, forget it," Frank teased as he came up behind his brother.

Joe sat down next to Scott and began to put on his skates. "Is Kevin coming?" he asked. "I hope he's still not mad at us."

"He said he'd definitely meet us here. In fact, he was the one who suggested Young's Pond," Scott told the Hardys. "I managed to cool him down yesterday, but I think he's still hurt that you guys suspect him of setting those fires. By the way," he added, "how's your investigation going?"

"Pretty slowly," Frank said evasively, with a warning glance at Joe. Until they knew who was responsible for the fires, it was important not to talk about the arson evidence they'd found to anyone except the police or the fire chief.

Scott laughed. "That doesn't surprise me," he said. "Not because you guys aren't good detectives," he added hastily, "but because there probably isn't anything to investigate. I think Pierce is just trying to cover up his mistakes." Scott grabbed his hockey stick and skated out onto the ice.

Taking Scott's lead, Frank slid onto the ice, pushing all thoughts of the case from his mind and concentrating on hockey. Joe appeared beside him a moment later, and the three of them began to hit the puck around to one another. Then they took turns playing two on one. When it was Joe's turn to play by himself, Scott cried, "Try blocking this one, Hardy!" He gave the puck a whack that sent it sliding past Joe down the length of the pond.

"I'll get you for that, Malone!" shouted Joe.

Frank chuckled as his brother skated furiously after the puck. Then a loud *crack!* rang out into the winter air, and Frank suddenly tensed. The ice! he realized. It was too thin to support Joe's weight! It was making loud cracking noises, but Frank could see that his brother was moving too fast to stop.

"Look out!" he called to Joe.

But it was too late. Even as he yelled the warning, there was the sickening sound of breaking ice and a cry for help.

"Oh, no!" Frank shouted. "Joe's fallen through the ice!"

5 Warning: Thin Ice

Frank took off over the ice toward his brother. "We've got to get him out of that freezing water!" he called back to Scott.

When Frank reached Joe, stopping several feet away from the hole in the ice, he saw him thrashing around in the water. Chunks of ice floated around him. Frank's mind was racing. Joe would freeze if he didn't get him out of that icy water—and fast! He hoped the ice would withstand his weight if he stretched out flat on it. Tossing his hockey stick to Joe, Frank lay across the ice and yelled, "Hold tight."

"I got it," Joe told him through chattering teeth. "Get me out of here."

Frank dug the front of his ice-skate blades into the ice to try to get a grip, but he couldn't dig them in deep enough. "Scott, I need your help," Frank called frantically.

"I'm right behind you, Frank," Scott called out. "I'll hold on to you." Scott knelt down and grasped Frank's ankles.

Frank and Scott slowly inched their way back from the hole. Frank held on to his end of the hockey stick tightly, but Joe's frozen fingers were almost too numb to move.

"Come on, Joe, hold *on*," Frank urged. Joe grimaced and gave it all the strength he could muster, and gradually Frank and Scott pulled him out of the water.

"Joe, are you okay?" Frank asked, looking over at his brother, whose lips had turned blue. All three of them were lying on their backs, gasping from the effort.

Joe felt as if icy fingers had squeezed all the air out of his lungs and pierced his hands and feet with cold, sharp needles. He winced at the pain as Frank quickly removed his skates and socks and began to rub his feet. But gradually the feeling returned to his feet and toes.

"Do you feel numb anywhere else?" Frank asked him anxiously.

Joe shook his head. "Just wet," he replied. He propped himself up on his elbows and wiggled his toes experimentally. "I'm fine now. My teeth have even stopped chattering." He looked at Frank and Scott. "You guys okay?"

They both nodded. "Good thing you weren't in the water that long," Scott said. Looking toward the bank straight ahead of him, Scott saw Kevin approaching through the trees. They all said hello and explained to Kevin what had happened. Kevin walked over to the opposite bank and brought over the socks and boots that had been left there in a pile.

"Hey," said Frank, looking at the others. "Why isn't there a sign posted warning skaters about thin ice?"

"Good question," said Kevin, handing each of them their socks and boots. "This is a town pond. The police department should have put up a sign."

"Who cares about signs," Joe muttered. He put on his socks and boots, then slowly got to his feet. "I just want to get home and into some dry clothes." He turned to the others. "Thanks, guys, for getting me out of there."

"Can you feel your fingers and toes?" Kevin asked.

"No problem," Joe said. "I always wanted to go for a swim in January."

While Joe, Kevin, and Scott began to trudge through the snow toward the path that led to the street, Frank walked toward some footprints he'd spotted in the snow. Bending down, he glimpsed a thick piece of wood half-buried under the snow and dead leaves. Curious, he pulled out the wood and picked up two small metal nails that had been lying under it. He nodded grimly when he saw what was written on the wood: "Warning— Thin Ice. Bayport Police Department."

Frowning, he turned and headed after the others.

Scott and Kevin had already left by the time Frank reached the end of the path. Joe was inside the Hardys' van, trying to warm up.

"Take a look at what I found in the woods," Frank said.

Joe stared in surprise at the warning sign Frank held up.

"I found these lying under the sign," Frank went on, digging into his jacket pocket and pulling out two shiny nails. "They fit the holes at the top and bottom of the wood. Someone deliberately removed the nails and the sign and hid them."

"What kind of jerk would do something like that?" Joe demanded indignantly.

"Maybe someone who wanted us to skate here," Frank said quietly. "Someone suspected of arson who hoped we'd have an 'accident' that would get us off the Pierce case."

"You think Kevin did it," Joe said, his expression darkening.

"He was the one who suggested skating here," Frank pointed out.

"But I can't believe—"

The van's phone began to ring, and Joe reached down to pick up the receiver. Frank raised his eyebrows in surprise as he heard his brother say, "We'll be happy to give you a few minutes of our time, Mr. Dawson. . . . Right. We'll be down there in half an hour."

"So why does Dawson want to see us?" Frank asked after his brother had hung up.

Joe shrugged. "He didn't say, but I'm definitely curious."

Half an hour later Joe had changed into dry clothes, and he and Frank had made the short drive to the offices of the *Bayport Examiner*.

"Mr. Dawson is expecting us. We're Frank and Joe Hardy," Frank said to the young man sitting at the receptionist's desk. On the wall behind his desk hung a big metal plaque with the newspaper's logo on it—a huge magnifying glass—next to the words *Bayport Examiner*, which were spelled out in bold blue letters.

The man consulted a list on his desk and nodded. "Oh, yes. You can go right in." He pointed to a door on his right. "His office is through that door, at the end of the newsroom. You can't miss it."

Frank pushed open the door, and an explosion of noise and activity greeted him. For a moment he just looked around the newsroom, taking everything in. People were talking loudly to each other or on the telephone, hurrying in and out of offices, moving quickly from desk to desk. Phones rang, typewriters clacked, computers beeped, and printers and fax machines hummed.

Frank spotted Callie sitting at a desk off to the left. She met his gaze and immediately pointed to an empty desk near hers. Then she silently mouthed the word "Maguire."

Frank nodded and gave her the thumbs-up sign. Callie was definitely close enough to the reporter's desk to keep a close eye on him.

Frank and Joe walked through the newsroom, past desk after desk, to a glassed-in office with Sam Dawson's name printed in big letters on the door. Just as Joe was about to knock on the door, it opened.

Joe found himself facing a handsome man with curly brown hair and piercing blue eyes. He looked to be in his mid-forties, Joe guessed, and he was casually dressed in khaki pants and a tweed jacket.

"You must be Frank and Joe Hardy," the man

50

said heartily, smiling and extending his hand. "I'm Sam Dawson."

"I'm Frank Hardy, and this is my brother, Joe," said Frank. They shook hands with the newspaper owner, then followed him into his office.

"Please sit down," Dawson said, motioning to two leather chairs in front of his desk, which was piled high with a confusion of printouts, newspaper clippings, and memos.

"You two must be wondering why I asked you to see me," Dawson said as he sat behind the desk. "Well, I'll come straight to the point." He leaned forward and folded his hands on the top of his desk. "I understand from Mark Maguire that you're investigating an arson case for Donald Pierce," he said.

Joe and his brother exchanged a wary glance. Then Joe turned to Dawson and said calmly, "Assuming that's true, Mr. Dawson, why is it any of your business?"

"Maybe your investigation isn't any of my business," Dawson said. "But I've met your father several times. He's a fine man. I simply can't believe that the sons of Fenton Hardy would agree to work for a lowlife like Pierce. If you continue to work for him, your credibility as detectives could be seriously damaged. I wouldn't want to see that happen."

"Thanks for your concern, Mr. Dawson," Frank said quietly. "But we're not going to stop investigating. *If* the fires were arson, then there's an arsonist out there who needs to be caught before he strikes again."

"What have you got against Pierce anyway?" Joe asked the newspaper owner. "I know he doesn't have a great reputation, but there are lots of lousy landlords out there. Why pick on Pierce?"

"I'll tell you why," Dawson said evenly, gazing intently at Frank and Joe. "I'm against real-estate people like Donald Pierce and everything they stand for—money, power, and greed. Pierce is by far the worst landlord and the most corrupt businessman in town, and I have a professional responsibility to make sure my readers know it!"

"And if you barbecue Pierce long enough in the *Examiner*, maybe his reputation will be ruined and he'll be history in Bayport," guessed Frank.

"Exactly," Dawson said. "I've got Mark Maguire on the story." He shook his head and added in an admiring tone, "Mark's my best investigative reporter. I'm really grateful he decided to leave the *Chronicle* in Washington, D.C., to come here."

"You know, I'm really surprised Pierce hasn't sued you for defamation of character," Joe put in.

"And I'd hate to think what he'd do to you *and* the *Examiner* if he ever found out that Maguire had been spying on him."

Dawson leaned back in his chair, a confident smile on his face. "Pierce would never sue me or the *Examiner*," he said softly. "Not in a million years."

Frank was surprised at Dawson's smug tone. Glancing at his watch, he realized that he and Joe were due at the firehouse in just ten minutes for a drill. "We have to be going now," Frank said to Dawson, getting up from his chair. "Thanks for the advice. It's too bad we can't take it."

"Suit yourself," Dawson said. He stood up and rounded the desk to the door. "But if you're determined to continue your investigation, here's a tip for you: It wouldn't surprise me in the least if Pierce set those fires himself, just to get the insurance money. Consider it." He smiled as he ushered them out the door.

"Dawson sounds like he's out to get Pierce," Joe commented as he and Frank climbed into the van. "I wonder why he's so sure that Pierce won't retaliate by suing him." He turned to his brother. "Do you think he has something on Pierce?"

"Could be," Frank said as they drove down the street toward the firehouse. "But what?" He thought for a minute, then suggested, "Maybe Pierce *is* torching his own buildings to collect the

53

insurance money, like Dawson says, and is setting up Kevin to divert suspicion from himself."

"It's a possibility," said Joe. "But if he's the arsonist, why did he hire us to investigate the fire in the first place?"

"I don't know," admitted Frank. "But I think we ought to find out more about Pierce's operation, don't you?"

"Absolutely," agreed Joe. "What we need is a spy inside Pierce's office." Joe grinned. "And we've got the perfect person—Iola! I'll call her tonight. I'm sure she can do it!"

When the Hardys reached the firehouse, Chief Sullivan was already starting to address the group of volunteer fire fighters about the practice drill.

Joe glanced around as he listened to the chief give instructions. A few fire fighters were missing, he noticed, including Kevin and Scott.

Sullivan rumbled on in his deep voice a while longer, then said, "Okay, guys, the drill starts *now*. Get moving. And remember, I'm timing you!"

Joe and the other fire fighters sprang into action, putting on their protective clothing, adjusting their air packs, and making sure the hoses, ladders, and fire extinguishers were secure on the trucks. Then they quickly boarded the engines.

Suddenly the red phone in the firehouse rang, and the chief picked up the receiver.

"At least the caller has good timing," Joe cracked, but his expression grew serious when he saw the grim look on Sullivan's face.

"Burning garage!" the chief shouted, slamming down the phone. Then he barked out the address.

Joe looked at his brother in horror.

"That's *our* garage!" he cried. "Aunt Gertrude was going to clean in there. She could be trapped inside!"

6 Firebombed

Frank hung on tight to the fire engine as it sped down the streets of Bayport behind the hook and ladder truck, sirens wailing. The fire chief and fire inspector followed, the red light on top of their car flashing brightly.

"Come *on*," Joe muttered anxiously beside his brother. "Why is it taking so long to get there?"

"It just seems that way," Frank replied. He tried to sound calm, but he could feel beads of sweat forming on his forehead, and he was gripping his pry bar so tightly that the muscles in his hand were beginning to ache.

Finally the engines pulled up to the curb in front of the Hardys' house. While the fire fighters grabbed canisters off the engines, Frank and Joe looked frantically around the yard for their aunt. Frank spotted her standing on the porch of their next-door neighbor's house. The neighbor, a middle-aged woman, had her arm around Aunt Gertrude.

"She's okay," Frank called to Joe, breathing a heavy sigh of relief.

Without wasting a moment, Frank hurried over to the engine, grabbed a fire extinguisher, and carried it as close as he could to the blazing garage. The aluminum door was raised, and he was relieved to see that the fire didn't seem to have reached the house. Aiming the nozzle, he began to douse the flames.

Frank and the other fire fighters worked quickly, and within fifteen minutes the fire was out. Then Frank and Joe, Chief Sullivan, and the fire inspector cautiously stepped into the burned-out shell and began to look around.

"I found something," Joe called out a few moments later. Frank saw his brother lean over and pick up a curved, soot-blackened piece of glass that had been lying on the concrete floor. Part of a label was still visible on the glass. "A beer bottle," Joe said, reading the label. He looked at the others. "Nobody in our family drinks beer," he said.

"Let me see that," the fire inspector said. Joe

handed him the broken bottle, and the inspector sniffed it. "Gasoline," he said. "Of course, I'll have to send it to the lab, but I'm pretty sure of what it is."

Frank came over to get a closer look at the glass. "It's a piece of a Molotov cocktail," he said. "Also known as a firebomb."

"Right," said the inspector. "Someone filled a beer bottle with gasoline, stuffed a gasoline-soaked rag in the top, lit the rag, and threw the device into your garage. A crude but effective bomb," he added.

Sullivan looked at the Hardys, a puzzled expression on his bearded face. "Why would someone want to firebomb your garage?" he asked them.

Joe shot his brother a look and answered, "We're not quite sure, sir." Both he and Frank were reluctant to tell the chief anything while others could be listening.

"I think we'd better go see how Aunt Gertrude is doing," Frank said. "Maybe she'll have some information for us. We'll let you know what we find out."

But he and Joe soon discovered that their aunt didn't know much. All she could tell them was that she had been in the kitchen when she heard the sound of breaking glass and a small explosion.

When she looked out the window, she saw flames in the garage.

"I called the fire department and then ran over to Mrs. Garofolo's house," Aunt Gertrude concluded. "This is awful, just awful," she wailed. "What will your parents say?"

"They'll cope," Joe said, patting his aunt's shoulder.

After making sure their aunt had calmed down, Joe and Frank rode the fire engine back to the fire station to get their van. It wasn't until they were at the firehouse that Joe noticed Kevin had joined the fire fighters. Kevin had already taken off his gear and was leaning against one of the fire engines in a sleeveless flannel shirt, his bare, muscular arms folded across his chest.

Joe did a double-take when he saw Kevin's shirt. Reaching into his jacket pocket, he pulled out the piece of flannel he had pocketed at the warehouse. He looked at the swatch, then at Kevin's shirt. The colors and patterns matched perfectly! Joe gave his brother a poke and silently showed him what he had discovered.

Frank's brown eyes opened wide. "It really looks bad for Kevin now," he whispered. "His flannel shirt and the matching swatch make for some pretty incriminating evidence."

"Not to mention that whoever firebombed our

garage had to have done it while we were at the drill—the drill Kevin missed," Joe added dejectedly.

"We still don't have concrete proof he *did* do it," Frank pointed out. "But for now, we'd better get back to Aunt Gertrude. After what happened, I don't think it's a good idea to leave her alone for too long."

When the Hardys got home, the fire-blackened garage was silhouetted against the setting sun. They tried to avoid looking at it as they walked up the path to the house.

"Hey, what's this?" Joe asked as he checked the mailbox. Pulling out a piece of paper, he unfolded it and read what was written on it.

"Another love letter?" guessed Frank.

"You got it," Joe replied, and read the note out loud. " 'You guys just aren't getting the message. You'd better mind your own business, or next time you'll be out of business—permanently.' "

"Are you thinking what I'm thinking?" asked Frank.

Joe nodded. "I'm thinking we'd better find out who this guy is—and fast!"

Early the next morning Frank called his father in Washington, D.C. When he had gotten off the kitchen phone, he walked into the den, where Joe was lying on the couch watching TV.

"Did you talk to Dad?" Joe asked, flicking off the TV with the remote control.

Frank nodded. "I filled him in and asked him to get us any information he could on Maguire's background. He said he'd do some digging for us. I also told him about the garage," he added.

"What did he say?" Joe asked, sitting up.

Frank shrugged. "He wasn't too thrilled, understandably. He just told us to be careful."

Just then the doorbell rang. Frank left the den and headed for the front hall. As soon as he opened the door, Con Riley stepped past him into the house.

"Okay," Con said, striding to the living room and sitting on the sofa. "Fill me in. I just talked to Chief Sullivan. What was that firebomb all about?"

"We wanted to tell you first, Con," Frank said, sitting down next to the lieutenant while Joe perched on the arm of a chair. "We were going to call you this morning, honest."

"Okay," said Con with a nod, "but now I want to hear the *whole* story."

Frank told him about their investigation. When he had finished, Con asked, "Got any suspects yet?"

"Well, there's Kevin Thomas," Frank told him. "He's a volunteer fire fighter who used to work for Pierce as a super. Pierce fired him and thinks he set the fires to get revenge."

"Then there's Mark Maguire, a reporter for the *Bayport Examiner*," Frank continued. "Through a very creative investigative technique, he heard us say we were going to the first warehouse that burned to look for clues."

"We're considering Pierce as a suspect, too," Joe added. "He could have burned his own buildings to get the insurance money."

Con thought for a minute. Then he stood up, shaking his head. "Well, I'm tempted to insist that you guys get off the case," he said. "Catching an arsonist is dangerous business."

"Come on, Con," said Joe. "You know we can handle it."

"Okay," Con relented as he started for the door. "Just be careful." He opened the door, then turned back to the Hardys and said, "And from now on, keep me posted, okay?"

"You bet, Con," Frank said. "You'll let the fire chief know what's going on?"

"It's a deal," Con answered, then left.

After Frank had shut the door, Joe asked, "Where do we go from here?"

Frank thought for a moment. "We still need to check out those other buildings that burned," he said. "But first, let's pay a visit to the apartment building where Kevin was the super. I think we should check out his story about being fired."

"Good idea," said Joe. "We can get the address from Iola. And I can ask her to check up on Pierce for us, too."

Iola answered the phone on the second ring. Joe quickly told her about the possibility that Pierce had set fire to his own buildings. "We want you to do a little spying for us, Iola. See if you can find out anything about Pierce's financial situation—you know, whether he's in good shape or not."

"Okay," she told him in an excited voice. "I'll see what I can dig up for you."

"And another thing," continued Joe. "Do you have the address of the apartment building where Kevin Thomas was the super?"

"Sure," Iola replied. "Hang on while I check." A moment later she came back on the line and told him, "It's Two twenty-five Sycamore Street."

Joe repeated the address out loud, then thanked Iola and hung up the phone.

"Let's go!" he called to Frank, grabbing his jacket and heading outside to the van.

There was still a little slush on the road, and Joe negotiated the van carefully toward Sycamore Street. As he turned off the engine and got out of the van, he took a good look at the small apartment building.

It was a brick building six stories high, with trash-strewn empty lots on either side of it, and another vacant lot behind it. The front of the building was crisscrossed with fire escapes.

"You know, the front of this place looks newer and more solid than the sides," commented Frank as they walked up to the building. "Pierce must have renovated only the front. I wonder why he didn't fix up the rest?"

"That's easy," replied Joe. "He probably didn't want to spend the money."

Joe tried the door. The lock was broken, and it opened easily.

"This place is a slum," he said in disgust, glancing around. Paint and plaster were peeling off the walls, and there were holes in the foyer rug. The hall lights were burned out, and there was a big Out of Order sign on the elevator.

"I thought Kevin had that fixed," Frank said. "Come on, let's start knocking on doors."

Half an hour later Frank and Joe were climbing the stairs from the fifth to the sixth floor. Out of the entire first five floors, they had talked to only five tenants. The others weren't home.

"This is getting weird," said Joe. "Everyone we've talked to either said what a great guy Pierce is or shut the door in our faces. And none of them seemed to remember Kevin at all!"

"Well, let's see what this person has to say," Frank said. He knocked on a door marked 6-B.

"I wouldn't bother if I were you," said a voice from behind the Hardys. "He's not home. Nobody on this floor is . . . except me, that is. Most of the tenants in this building are at work."

Joe turned and saw a tiny, white-haired woman smiling at them from the doorway of an apartment in the front of the building. She was holding an orange-colored tabby cat in her arms.

"In that case, maybe you can help us, ma'am," said Frank. "We're trying to get some information on Kevin Thomas and Donald Pierce." Joe followed his brother down the hall toward her, and the woman motioned for them to come in.

"Do sit down," she said as she settled into an easy chair, her cat in her lap. She scratched the cat behind one of its ears, and Joe could hear it purring. "Now, you wanted to know about Kevin, didn't you? And about my landlord, Donald Pierce." She frowned. "I'll bet the tenants you talked to told you what a wonderful man Mr. Pierce is."

"That's right, ma'am," said Joe. "Is that what you think?"

"I think he's a *terrible* landlord," the woman replied shortly. "He never fixes anything because he's too cheap and greedy. He told us he wouldn't increase our rent if we kept quiet about the reason he fired Kevin. Mind you, we knew why Kevin had been fired. One of the tenants overheard them yelling, and, well, news travels fast in a small apartment building like this one."

She smiled again. "Such a nice boy, Kevin, and what a good super! He had that elevator fixed right away. Of course, it's broken again now," she added with a sigh.

The woman looked at Frank and Joe. "Was that what you young men wanted to know?"

"Yes it is, ma'am," Frank said, grinning. "Thank you very much. You've been a big help."

He and Joe got up from the sofa. Suddenly Joe felt the floor of the apartment trembling, and he reached out to steady himself. A split second later a deafening crash shook the entire building. The woman clutched her cat and looked terror stricken. Joe could see that she was trembling.

Then, as suddenly as it started, the noise stopped. Joe and Frank raced out of the apartment, with Joe in the lead. Halfway down the hall, Joe stopped short so suddenly that Frank bumped into him. Joe stared straight ahead. "I don't believe what I'm seeing," he whispered.

About ten yards from where he and Frank were standing, the hallway simply ended. Where the back of the building had been, Joe now saw trees and blue sky. Looking down, he saw a huge pile of rubble and broken furniture.

Half the building had collapsed!

7 Danger Zone

"Come on," Frank said, grabbing his brother's arm. "We've got to call for help!"

"First we better get everyone out of the front apartments. The rest of this building could collapse any minute!" said Joe in an urgent voice.

He and Frank raced back into the elderly woman's apartment and quickly explained the situation to her. She listened tensely, then said, "I'm the only one in a front apartment on this floor who's home today, and there's just Mrs. Flores and Mr. Barnes on the third and fourth floors."

The woman put on her coat, placed her cat in its carrier, and handed the carrier to Joe. Frank

68

helped the white-haired woman climb out the living-room window onto the fire escape. Joe followed with the cat, who was meowing loudly in the cat carrier. As they began to climb down the metal stairs, Joe spotted a man on the fire escape a few stories below. He was helping a woman climb out one of the front windows.

"Those are the two people I told you about," said the elderly woman a bit breathlessly. "Thank goodness they realized what's happened!"

When the Hardys, the elderly woman, and the cat were safely on the ground, Joe ran across the street to a small grocery store to phone the fire department and the police.

Frank hurried around to the back of the apartment building, his adrenaline pumping. He had to work quickly if he hoped to rescue anyone trapped in the rubble. Carefully he picked his way over the pieces of brick and plaster, listening for any signs of life.

Suddenly he froze. Was that . . . ? Yes! It was the faint cry of help coming from an area of rubble off to his left.

Frank scrambled up the pile of rubble in the direction of the voice and began to pull away pieces of debris. Soon he had uncovered the face, chest, and arms of a man. Frank let out a sigh of relief as the man blinked up at him. There were cuts and bruises on his face, but when Frank checked his pulse, it was normal, and he appeared to be breathing steadily.

Having been trained in first aid, Frank knew it would be better if he didn't try to move the man. He could have broken bones that could be injured more by being moved.

"An ambulance should be here any minute," he told the man in a reassuring voice. "Just lie quietly and try to relax, okay?"

The man gave a slight nod and whispered hoarsely, "Thanks."

Sirens screamed in the distance, faintly at first, then louder and louder. Giving the man an encouraging smile, Frank said, "I'll tell the rescuers where you are," then turned and hurried back down the rubble. As he ran around to the front of the building, he saw a police car barreling down the street, followed by a fire engine, Chief Sullivan's red car, and two ambulances.

"I called the gas company, too," Joe said, coming up to his brother. "There are probably leaking gas pipes in that building. We don't want an explosion on our hands!"

By now a curious crowd had gathered around the building. "Please step back out of the way," Frank called out loudly and firmly. "The rescue teams will need all the room they can get." He and Joe began to herd the crowd of people away from the building.

Scott was among the several fire fighters who jumped out of the engine armed with shovels, picks, and axes. They rushed around to the back of the building, followed by two police officers and some paramedics. One of the officers was holding tightly to the leash of the police department's German shepherd, Austin. Frank knew that Austin would be used to sniff out people trapped in the rubble.

"I thought I'd find you here." Frank and Joe turned to find Chief Sullivan standing behind them. "Want to fill me in on the situation?"

Frank quickly explained what had happened. When he had finished, Sullivan nodded grimly and said, "I've seen this kind of thing before. A landlord only renovates half of an old building to save money. That weakens the rest of the structure, which usually isn't too strong to begin with."

"Do you want us to help with the rescue, Chief?" asked Joe.

Sullivan shook his head. "We've got plenty of people on the job. You boys have been through enough already." He turned and strode off toward the rescue teams.

Finally the paramedics began to emerge from the rubble-strewn site carrying people on portable gurneys. Frank was thankful to see that so far they were all alive. The third gurney held the

71

man Frank had uncovered in the debris. His head was bandaged and one leg was in a splint. Frank went over to the two paramedics who were with the man.

"How are they?" Frank asked after the paramedics had positioned the gurney in the back of the ambulance and were getting ready to drive off.

"A lot of cuts and bruises, and some broken bones," one of them replied. "They're very lucky people. Their injuries could have been much more severe."

Frank felt his brother nudge him. "Look who's here," said Joe. "Our favorite reporter."

Frank turned and saw Mark Maguire talking to the fire chief and the two police officers. As he spoke, the reporter's gaze was roving over the area. When he spotted the Hardys, Maguire excused himself and walked up to them.

"You guys would make good reporters," he said with a grin. "You seem to know instinctively where to find a good story."

"Is that how you see this disaster?" Joe asked. "Just as a 'good story'?"

"Hey, don't get me wrong," Maguire said quickly. "I feel bad for these people, I really do. But I have to admit that this building collapse is giving me another great chance to show *Examiner* readers what a beast Pierce is. I'll do *anything* to get the dirt on him."

"Like follow him around," Frank put in. "To our house, for instance."

Maguire shrugged. "I'm sorry about that," he said, but Frank didn't think he sounded very sincere. "The Pierce story means a lot to me. It's going to raise me back up to the top of my profession—where I belong."

Frank didn't know why Maguire had slipped from the top of his profession in the first place. He made a mental note to find out as soon as possible what Callie had learned about Maguire's background. In the meantime, he decided to take a direct approach with the reporter.

"You haven't printed the conversation you heard Sunday morning outside our house yet," he said. "Are you going to?"

"It could seriously hurt our case if you did," Joe added.

Maguire laughed. "What case? The fires, just like the building collapse, were obviously accidents caused by a greedy, careless landlord. Pierce is just trying to save what's left of his reputation." The reporter continued to smile. "And you know what I think?" he returned calmly. "I think Pierce is paying you guys to conduct a phony investigation. I'd quit working on this so-called arson case if I were you," he said in a calm voice. "If you're not careful, your reputation will go right down the tubes with your friend Pierce's." He looked at the Hardys for a second longer, then turned and walked away.

"You know, it's interesting that both Maguire and Dawson have warned us off the case," commented Frank once the reporter was gone. "They even used the same reasons—they both insisted there's no case to investigate, and they're both convinced our reputations as detectives will be ruined."

"Yeah, I noticed that, too," said Joe. "What if they're setting the fires together?"

Frank thought for a moment. "Maguire said he'd do anything to get dirt on Pierce. Do you think he and Dawson would go so far as to commit arson at Pierce's properties to get news?"

"That would be pretty risky," said Joe.

He and Frank walked to their van and climbed in, with Joe in the driver's seat. "Maybe Kevin's not the arsonist," Joe suggested hopefully. "I mean, we know he's telling the truth about why he was fired. Maybe he has a good explanation about the flannel swatch that matches his shirt, too. Let's go over to his place now and talk to him."

Frank agreed, and twenty minutes later Joe turned the van onto Kevin's street, then parked it in front of a small ranch house in the middle of the block. Frank was concentrating so hard on the case that it wasn't until he was halfway up Kevin's driveway that he saw what was sitting there.

He stopped dead in his tracks. "Joe! It's a blue van!"

8 Suspicious
Secrets

Joe stared at the van in amazement.

"The question is," he said in a low voice, "does it belong to Kevin or to someone who's visiting him?"

"We'll find out soon enough," said Frank, getting out of the van.

"Wait a minute," said Joe, stepping over to the blue van to take a closer look. "No smudged license plate, no broken tail pipe. And the words *Bayport Examiner* are clearly printed in white lettering on both sides. . . . This can't be the one we followed on Sunday," he concluded with a frustrated sigh. "But what's an *Examiner* van doing here?"

"There's only one way to find out." Frank turned and walked toward the house, and Joe followed behind.

Kevin answered Frank's second knock on the door, When he saw the Hardys standing on the front steps, he looked warily at them.

"What do you guys want?" Kevin asked, his eyes darting back and forth between Frank and Joe. Joe noticed that he was still wearing the sleeveless flannel shirt that matched the swatch they had found at the warehouse.

"Look, Kevin," Frank said. "We want to help you. You've got to believe us."

"If you really want to help me, then stop suspecting me of arson," insisted Kevin. But he opened the door a little wider.

"The only way we can do that is if you cooperate with us," Joe said. "There are some questions we need you to answer."

Kevin looked from Frank to Joe, then he bit his lip and nodded. "Okay. Come on in."

The Hardys followed Kevin into the small living room, which held a few worn armchairs and a comfortable-looking sofa.

Kevin glanced at his watch as he sat down in one of the armchairs. "So what do you want to know?" he asked.

77

"First of all, what's an *Examiner* van doing parked in your driveway?" Joe asked.

"That's an easy one," Kevin said, smiling a little. "I got a part-time job delivering the paper for a friend who's sick. I've been having a tough time getting a full-time job, so right now I'm taking any work I can get. What else?"

"What did you mean when you said you'd 'get' Pierce?" Frank asked. He saw Kevin frown. "We have to know, Kevin," he added quietly.

Kevin looked down at the floor and sighed. "I guess it was really dumb of me to lose my temper and threaten him like that. I was mad at him, that's all. I didn't know what I was saying. That's the truth, guys." He raised his head to look at the Hardys, then glanced at his watch again.

Joe looked at Frank and then down at his jacket pocket. When his brother nodded, Joe pulled the flannel swatch out and held it out to Kevin. "This piece of material has been soaked in gasoline. We found it at the first Pierce warehouse that burned, along with other evidence of arson," he told Kevin. "Does it look familiar?"

Kevin's face went pale. "It's the same pattern as the shirt I'm wearing," he admitted nervously. "But if you're saying I cut off the arms of my shirt and used the pieces to start a fire, you're wrong." He fingered the armholes of his shirt. "One of the sleeves was ripped really badly, so I decided to cut both sleeves off and make a muscle shirt," he explained. "I used the sleeves as cleaning rags for a while, but then they got too dirty to wash, and I threw them away."

He looked at Frank and Joe, a pleading expression on his face. "Bob's Army-Navy Store was selling tons of these shirts during the holidays!" he cried. "*Anybody* could have this shirt!"

Kevin looked at his watch for the third time, then stood up. "Look, I've got to leave for an appointment, and I'm running late," he said quickly. "Is that all you guys wanted to know?"

Frank and Joe stood up and followed Kevin to the front door. "Just one more thing," said Frank as Kevin opened the door. "Why were you late for all three Pierce fires?"

Kevin's mouth dropped open. But then he snapped it shut again and shook his head. "Sorry, Frank, I can't tell you that," he said firmly. "At least, not now. All I'll say is that I had a good reason for showing up late."

"But what kind of reason could—" Joe started to say.

"I've really got to go now," Kevin interrupted. Then he ushered the Hardys outside and shut the door.

Once the Hardys were back in the van, Joe

turned to his brother and asked, "What do you think. Was he telling the truth?"

"What he *said* makes sense," Frank said slowly, "but he sure was *acting* pretty funny, and he's obviously hiding something." He shook his head. "I'm still not convinced Kevin's in the clear."

Just then the phone in the van rang. When Joe answered it, he heard Iola's voice say excitedly, "I finish work at three today. Can you guys meet me at the Bayport Diner in twenty minutes? I've got some information for you."

"Great!" said Joe. "We're on our way!"

When he and Frank got to the diner, Iola was already sitting in a booth at the back. She spotted them and waved.

"What have you got for us?" Joe asked her as he and Frank eased into the booth across from her. After they had all ordered burgers, fries, and sodas, Iola leaned toward the Hardys and said, "I eavesdropped on a meeting Pierce had with his accountant this morning. Pierce definitely has money trouble. In fact, he's had a big cash-flow problem for a while. He's sunk a lot of money into expensive developing projects, such as shopping centers and condos. But he needs more money, and banks haven't been too willing to lend it to him. They think he's a poor risk. Pierce blamed his situation on Sam Dawson and the *Examiner* articles. He said Dawson was definitely out to get him, but he didn't mention why."

"If Pierce needs money," Frank said thoughtfully, "that gives him a definite motive for planning those fires—to collect on the insurance."

"But then why would he hire you to investigate arson?" Iola asked in a puzzled tone.

"We haven't quite figured that one out yet," Joe told her.

"Oh," Iola said suddenly. "I just remembered something else. It's probably not important, but I heard Pierce say that sometimes he wished he were still working at some little bank in New Mexico. He said he wasn't as successful back then, but life was a lot less stressful."

Their food arrived, and Joe took a big bite out of his burger. "Well, he's going to feel a whole lot of stress if it turns out he's the arsonist," he commented.

"Do you guys want me to keep spying on Pierce for you?" asked Iola as she took a sip of her soda.

"Definitely," Frank told her. "I'm curious about his life in New Mexico and how he got to be such a success in Bayport. In fact, I'm surprised Dawson hasn't gotten Maguire to do some digging into Pierce's background. You'd think Dawson and Maguire would want to print information about Pierce's past."

81

"I'll see what I can find out," promised Iola.

"Great, Iola," Joe said, smiling at her. "Thanks."

Iola grinned back at Joe, her eyes sparkling. "No problem."

Suddenly the beeper in Frank's jacket went off. Frank pulled the beeper out of his pocket and switched it off. Then he left the booth and headed to the diner's pay phone. When he came back a few minutes later, Joe immediately spotted the anxious look on his face.

"We'd better hurry," Frank said urgently. "This is a bad one. An explosion in a warehouse caused a warehouse next to it to catch on fire. The engines are already on the way."

Joe shoved the last two fries into his mouth and slid out of the booth. He called goodbye to Iola and ran for the exit.

"The warehouse that exploded was the *second* Pierce warehouse that burned, the one we haven't checked out yet for arson," Frank explained. "Apparently, it's been totally leveled."

Joe jumped into the driver's seat and gunned the van's engine as Frank got in the other side. "I bet someone blew up the warehouse so we wouldn't be able to find any clues there," he said, frowning. He pulled out into the street.

Joe remembered that the warehouse was in an

older industrial area outside of Bayport, across the road from a state park, and he headed that way as fast as he could.

When they arrived at the scene of the fire, Frank and Joe hurried over to the engine. They grabbed their protective clothing and got into it quickly.

While Joe ran over to help man the hose, someone handed Frank an air pack from the truck. Without looking up, Frank took it and adjusted it on his back. Then he grabbed a fire extinguisher and began to run toward the blazing building. Ahead of him, the other fire fighters were circling around to the left side of the building to douse the flames at the back. Frank decided he'd better go around to the right side of the warehouse and see what he could do there.

The smoke became denser as Frank got closer to the building, and the heat grew more intense. Soon he was having trouble breathing. Pressing the air pack's mask to his face, he took a deep breath. Nothing. No oxygen was getting into the mask. He tried again, but all he breathed in was the same bitter, smoky air he'd breathed out.

Frank felt a sense of panic growing inside of him. The smoke was so thick that he couldn't see where he was going. His eyes were watering, and he was coughing and choking from a lack of oxygen. He tried to move away from the smoke, but he was beginning to feel so dizzy that he didn't know which way to go! Frantically he sucked at the mask again, then tore it off and tossed the useless thing aside.

Frank began to sway. His last thought before he lost consciousness was, I'm going to be burned alive!

9 The Masked Man

Joe squinted his eyes and peered worriedly toward the right side of the warehouse. Frank had disappeared in that direction over twenty minutes ago. Joe knew that his brother should have emptied his extinguisher and come back by now.

He turned to the fire fighter who was manning the hose with him. "Can you take over for me for a few minutes?" Joe asked. The fire fighter nodded and gripped a longer length of the hose as Joe stepped aside.

Grabbing an air pack from the engine, Joe jogged up to Alex Makeba, an older fire fighter who was trudging back from the warehouse carrying his empty canister.

"I think my brother's in trouble over there," he said quickly, motioning toward the warehouse. "I'm going after him, but he might need first aid, and you're the expert."

"Let's go," said Alex without hesitation.

The two of them adjusted their masks and started for the building. The flames had died down, but the thick smoke made it almost impossible to see. Suddenly Joe's foot caught on something lying on the ground, causing him to stumble. He looked down—and gasped. It was Frank! He was out cold, and he didn't even have his air mask on!

"Over here!" Joe called to Alex. The older man slid his hands under Frank's arms while Joe took hold of his brother's legs. They quickly carried Frank away from the dense smoke to a stretcher near one of the engines.

Alex immediately began to apply mouth-to-mouth resuscitation to Frank. After several anxious minutes Joe saw his brother's brown eyes blink open.

"What happened?" Frank asked in a hoarse voice. Then he burst into a spasm of coughing.

"Don't try to talk," warned Alex. "Just relax and concentrate on breathing normally." He turned to Joe. "He'll be okay, but I want you to give him oxygen. He's got some smoke in his lungs. I've got to go back and help finish off this fire."

As soon as Alex had left, Joe gently pressed an air-pack mask to his brother's face. After several breaths, the color had returned to Frank's face and he was breathing more easily. Propping himself up on one elbow, he told Joe what had happened to him.

"Either that air pack I was carrying was faulty or someone deliberately let the oxygen leak out of it," Frank concluded in a raspy voice. He reached for the mask and took another breath through it.

"Did you see who gave it to you?" asked Joe.

Frank shook his head and lowered the mask. "Everything was so hectic, I just took it without thinking."

Just then Chief Sullivan came up to them. Con Riley was with him.

"Are you okay?" Con asked Frank.

Frank nodded. "Thanks to Joe and Alex Makeba," he said. "My air pack was out of oxygen."

"What!" exclaimed Sullivan. "That's impossible. I checked every single air pack myself just before the fire was phoned in."

"Then it was sabotage," Joe concluded. "Someone must have let the oxygen out of the air pack while we were riding to the fire."

"Every one of my volunteers rode the engines," said Sullivan after a moment, "except for you two."

Joe shook his head. Could Kevin possibly be responsible for this? he wondered.

"It seems possible that an arsonist could have blown up this warehouse to hide any clues that might point to him," Chief Sullivan went on. "That's why I called Con out here."

"Do you two have any more leads on who's responsible?" Con asked Frank and Joe.

"Kevin could have set the explosion," Frank pointed out, looking up from the stretcher. "The timing was right. And he seemed pretty anxious to get rid of us when we talked to him this afternoon. He kept looking at his watch, and he practically shoved us out the door."

"And he said he had an appointment," added Joe. He looked at the lieutenant. "What do you think, Con?"

"He rode on the fire engine with everyone else," Chief Sullivan pointed out.

"Still, I don't think there's enough evidence yet to make an arrest," said Con. "Kevin could have been going anywhere. But maybe clues from the explosion will tell us something. I'd better go over and talk to the fire inspector."

He crouched down and gave Frank a pat on the

shoulder. "Go home and get some rest, Frank," he said. "I'll be in touch."

"Right, Con. Thanks," Frank said with a smile.

When Con and the fire chief had left, Frank swung his legs over the side of the stretcher and slowly stood up. He was leaning against the engine for support when Scott approached. His face was covered with sweat and black soot.

"Whew!" he said wearily, taking off his coat. "What a nightmare!" He reached into the engine and pulled out his leather jacket. "The smoke around that right side was really thick, but at least the fire's out now." He paused and stared at Frank.

"What happened to you?" asked Scott. "Did you get a lungful of smoke back there?"

"Something like that," Frank told him without going into detail.

Scott wiped his brow with his shirtsleeve, then put on his jacket. "You know, I probably shouldn't tell you guys this, since Kevin's my best friend," Scott said. "But something weird just happened. Kevin just took off. He was in a real hurry, said he had to take care of some business. He said he's leaving town tonight."

Frank and Joe looked at each other but didn't say anything.

After a short silence Scott said, "Well, I hope

you're okay, Frank." He turned and walked toward his sports car.

Frank waited in the van while Joe helped pack up the engines. Frank was feeling tired and was relieved when Joe hopped in the driver's seat and they finally were heading home.

"I'm going to drive over to Kevin's," Joe announced as they walked into their house. "If he's still home, maybe I can find out why he's leaving town."

"Good idea," Frank said. Taking off his jacket, he stretched out on the sofa and closed his eyes. "You don't mind if I stay here, do you?" he murmured drowsily.

"Are you kidding?" Joe said with a grin. "You'd probably fall asleep before we even got to the van!"

As he drifted off to sleep, Frank heard the front door open and close. He didn't know how long he had slept when he was awakened by the ringing of the doorbell. Still in a sleepy haze, he got up and answered the door.

Callie stepped into the house. "I've got some news for you," she said with a grin. Then her expression changed to one of concern. "What happened to you? You look terrible!"

Between yawns Frank told her. Then he flopped down in an easy chair and asked, "What have you got?"

"I've been watching your friend Maguire," Callie replied, sitting down on the sofa. "He's always out of the newsroom or in a private conference with Sam Dawson in Dawson's office. I don't know when he gets the time to write his stories."

"Maybe he writes them at home," guessed Frank. "Anything else?"

"Only that Dawson took the stringers out for lunch today," she reported. "He told us stories about his early days . . . you know, kind of as an inspiration to those of us who are new to the business. Anyway, he started out as a bank teller in New Mexico. Then he worked as a ranch hand in Texas and a stockbroker in New York City. Apparently, he made enough money on Wall Street to buy the *Examiner*."

Frank leaned forward in his chair. "You know, Iola told us that Pierce worked in a bank in New Mexico, too," he said slowly. "This might be a long shot, but I wonder if he and Dawson worked in the same bank."

"Maybe it's just a coincidence," said Callie, shrugging. "And anyway, even if they knew each other, what does that have to do with the fires?"

"I don't know, but it just might be a lead," replied Frank. "Do you think you could do some snooping around Dawson's office? Maybe you'll be able to find a clue in there that will link

Dawson and Pierce. Joe and I will ask Iola to check out Pierce's office, too."

"I'm going to the movies with Iola tonight. I can ask her, if you want," Callie said. "And I'll see what I can dig up in Dawson's office." She got up from the sofa. "If I were you, I'd take it easy, Frank. You look exhausted."

"Don't worry," Frank assured Callie. "As soon as you leave, I'm making a dive for the sofa!"

The sun was just setting when Joe arrived at Kevin's house. Kevin's car was parked in the driveway, but Joe noticed that the *Examiner* van was gone, and there didn't seem to be any lights on in the house.

Joe parked the van across the street, walked up to Kevin's front door, and rang the bell. When no one answered, he tried the door, but it was locked. Maybe this is a good time to do a little detective work inside the house, he thought. Moving around to the back of the house, Joe tested the door that led to the kitchen. It, too, was locked.

Looking to the right, Joe saw that there was a large window next to the kitchen door. He stepped over to it and tried pushing it open. The window raised easily.

With a quick glance to make sure no one was around, Joe hoisted himself up onto the sill and crawled through the window, landing on top of the sink. He dropped to the floor and began to look around, checking all the kitchen cabinets and drawers. Nothing. Then he searched the basement, but he didn't find anything suspicious there, either. There was a can of gasoline and some rags, but Joe knew that those could be found in anybody's home.

When Joe stepped into Kevin's bedroom, in his ranch house, the first thing he saw was a suitcase sitting on the floor. It looked as if Kevin was going somewhere, all right, but he hadn't left yet. Joe opened the suitcase and rifled through it, but it contained nothing except clothes and personal items.

All of a sudden Joe froze, listening carefully. The sound of footsteps crunching on ice was coming from somewhere near the house!

Joe quickly snapped the suitcase shut and hurried down the stairs to the living room. Glancing out the window, he saw a tall figure dressed in black and wearing a black-and-white ski mask running down the driveway. Joe raced to the front door, unlocked it, and ran out of the house after the person.

The figure in black glanced over his shoulder. When he saw Joe chasing him, he began to run faster. Joe picked up his pace, too, following the man as he turned left down a narrow, dead-end

93

street with a four-foot-high stone wall running along both sides of it.

Looking ahead, Joe saw that the blue van was parked at the end of the street. He was still twenty yards away from the van when the masked man jumped in. A second later the engine roared to life, and the van's bright lights flicked on, highlighting Joe like a target.

Joe stopped short as he realized what was about to happen. He didn't have time to turn around, because just then, with a squeal of its tires, the van shot forward straight at Joe!

10 The Case Heats Up

For a second Joe could only stare at the blinding headlights bearing down on him. Then, spinning around, he raced for the wall and hurtled over it head first, hoping that whatever was on the other side wasn't dangerous. A moment later he landed with a thud in a mound of snow.

Joe heard the van screech to a stop on the other side of the wall. Jumping to his feet, he turned in time to see the van zoom away down the street.

"Rats!" muttered Joe. It was the closest he'd come to seeing the person in the blue van, but he still couldn't identify who it was. "Next time I'll catch you, whoever you are," Joe said between his teeth as he climbed back over the wall.

He jogged down the street, letting out another groan when he got to Kevin's house. The house was still dark—but Kevin's car was gone. Joe had missed his chance to find out why Kevin was leaving.

Joe sighed. There was nothing else for him to do but go home.

When he walked in the front door ten minutes later, he glanced into the kitchen and heard Frank talking on the phone.

"Thanks for the information, Dad. We'll see you in a few days," Frank said, and hung up the phone.

"Did Dad find out anything about Maguire?" Joe asked, settling into a chair at the kitchen table.

Frank nodded. "It seems that our hotshot reporter was fired from the *Chronicle* in D.C. There was a rumor going around down there that some senator was taking bribes. Apparently, Maguire had some bad sources, and he never checked their information. He printed stuff that turned out to be false, and the senator sued the paper. That's why Maguire was canned."

Joe tapped his fingers on the table, remembering how Sam Dawson had praised Maguire, calling him his top reporter. "Dawson must have known about his past when he hired him," Joe commented.

"Probably," said Frank. "He might have jumped at the chance to hire a reporter who wouldn't check facts about Pierce too carefully. But wait, Joe, there's more. Dad told me that before Maguire got the Senate beat, he covered fires for the paper. He spent all his time with the D.C. fire department. He hung out with the fire fighters, was on the scene of every fire, and was friendly with the fire commissioner and fire inspector."

Joe sat up straight in his chair. "So Maguire has to know all about setting fires," he said excitedly.

"But even if he is responsible for the fires, he has to have an accomplice in the fire department," Frank reminded his brother. "It had to have been a fire fighter who let the oxygen out of my pack. That means Kevin's still a suspect. How did it go at Kevin's?" he asked.

"I didn't get to talk to him, but I had another little run-in with the blue van." Joe told Frank what had happened at Kevin's. "I don't think the guy in the van could have been Kevin," he concluded. "When I first got to Kevin's house, his car was there, but only a minute after the van almost ran me down, I got back to Kevin's and saw his car was gone. He couldn't have driven both cars at the same time."

"That's true, but it could have been whoever he's working with, maybe Maguire," Frank pointed out.

Joe shook his head. "I don't know. In spite of all the evidence, I still can't believe Kevin's responsible," he insisted. "There are a lot of fire fighters. Why don't we ask Con to check into them?"

"Good idea," Frank agreed. "Maybe one of the guys will leap out as a suspect."

"Let's do it first thing tomorrow," said Joe with a yawn. "It's been a long day. Right now I want to get some dinner. And then I'm planning to do some serious TV watching!"

It was eleven-thirty by the time Frank was up and dressed the next morning. Feeling fresh and completely recovered from the previous day's accident, he came down the stairs to find Joe lying on the sofa reading the front page of the *Examiner*.

"I don't believe what I'm seeing," Frank said in mock amazement. "My brother reading the front page instead of the sports page!"

Joe ignored Frank's comments. "You know, it's interesting," he said, sitting up. "There's nothing in the paper about yesterday's explosion and fire, but the building collapse gets heavy coverage.

Maguire makes Pierce come off as a real villain again."

Frank nodded. "That doesn't surprise me. Anyway, the collapse *was* Pierce's fault. Maybe this time he deserves the bad press."

The phone rang, and Frank headed into the kitchen to answer it. When he came back into the living room a few minutes later, he said, "That was Callie. She wants us to meet her and Jen Buckley for lunch. She has some more news for us."

"What do you mean, *more* news?" Joe asked in a puzzled tone.

Frank told his brother about the conversation he had had with Callie the evening before about Dawson's past. "It may not lead to anything," he finished with a shrug. "But you never know."

An hour later Frank and Joe drove to downtown Bayport and parked in front of a diner. "Burgerworks," Joe said, reading the sign over the entrance. "Hey, this is a new burger place!" he exclaimed, hopping quickly out of the van.

Frank grinned. "Callie chose it with you in mind."

When the brothers stepped into the diner, they joined Callie and Jen, who were sitting at a table near the window.

"I don't know about this place," Joe said

doubtfully as he scanned the menu. "One of the specialties is a 'Soy Joy Burger.'"

"They have regular burgers, too," said Jen, smiling at Joe. Her long blond hair curled around her shoulders and her blue eyes shone. She seemed to have gotten over some of the trauma of her home burning, Frank thought.

"How are your mother and Matt?" he asked her.

"They're doing okay," replied Jen. "And Pierce is planning to start renovating the house soon. My mom says that's the least he can do after being so negligent."

After the four of them had ordered, Callie said, "I wanted to tell you that I heard a fight between Maguire and Dawson this morning. Maguire thinks the Pierce story is getting stale, and he wants to give it a rest. I heard him say he's been printing more opinions than facts lately."

"What did Dawson say?" asked Frank.

"He insisted the story was helping to sell papers," Callie replied. "Then he said he wouldn't rest until Pierce's reputation was totally destroyed. That's all I heard."

Joe looked at his brother. "Maybe Maguire's afraid people will find out about his being fired from his job in D.C. if he keeps the Pierce story going," he suggested.

"Or maybe Maguire's just worried that we're

on his trail," Frank suggested. "If he's one of the arsonists, that is."

"We still need some real proof that Maguire's guilty," Joe said, shaking his head. Then he snapped his fingers and said to Frank, "I think it's time we looked for clues at Jen's house."

"That's a good idea," Frank said. "We planned to go over there, but things kept coming up and we never got around to it."

After lunch Frank and Joe headed over to the police station to update Con Riley. "I checked for records on Kevin, Maguire, Dawson, and Pierce," the lieutenant told the Hardys after they'd filled him in, "but they're clean."

"We'd like you to check on the fire fighters, too," Frank told Con. "I know it's a big job," he added hastily.

"Hey," Con said seriously. "No job is too big when you're trying to catch an arsonist. What concerns me is the fact that Kevin left town. That plus the swatch matchup make him a pretty strong suspect." He looked sternly at Frank and Joe. "I know he's your friend, but I'm going to have to find him and bring him in for questioning. I'm sorry, guys."

Frank and Joe stood silently for a moment. Then Frank nodded and said, "That's okay, Con, we understand."

Frank and Joe headed for the Buckleys' house after leaving Con. The windows of the fire-blackened house had been boarded up, and a rope with red flags attached to it circled the property.

"We'd better be careful walking inside the house," cautioned Frank as he and Joe got out of the van and stepped over the rope. "The wood might be weak because of the fire. We don't want to cause a collapse."

"No kidding," said Joe, carefully opening the front door to the Buckleys' apartment. "One building collapse in a week is enough for me!"

Frank and Joe searched the Buckleys' apartment, but there was no sign of arson. Then they searched through the apartment next door.

"There's old, frayed wiring all through this house," Joe said as they cautiously climbed down the stairs from the second floor. "But nothing we've seen so far points to arson."

"Keep checking in here," said Frank. "I'm going to look for clues outside."

Heading out the door, Frank circled around to the back of the house, looking closely at the walls and ground. He noticed that each apartment had a window in the foundation set into a well just below ground level.

He knelt down and looked in the well in front of the window on the Buckleys' side. He spotted a large, partly charred piece of blue fabric at the bottom of the well. Reaching down, he pulled it out. The piece of fabric looked to Frank as if it had once been a T-shirt, and the unmistakable smell of gasoline came from it.

Frank let out a low whistle. The fire had been arson, all right, and it looked as if it had been set the same way as the warehouse fire.

He paused, hearing footsteps on the ground behind him. "Hey, Joe," Frank called without turning around. "You'll never guess—"

Then Frank felt something hit him on the head, and everything went black.

11 Getting the Scoop

Joe sighed with frustration as he came out of the apartment next to the Buckleys'. He hadn't found a thing indicating arson, but maybe Frank had come up with something. He started around the outside of the building and stopped short. Frank was lying on the ground, and Mark Maguire was standing over him!

Leaping forward, Joe gave a yell of rage and rushed at the reporter.

"Hey!" Maguire shouted in protest as Joe grabbed his jacket and pulled the reporter toward him. Maguire tried to break free, but Joe was holding him in an iron grip.

"Why did you knock my brother out?" Joe demanded angrily. The reporter didn't answer.

Joe looked over at his brother and was relieved to see Frank's eyes had opened. "You okay, Frank?" he called over.

"Yeah." Frank rolled to his side and got slowly to his feet. "Let him go, Joe," he said quietly. "We don't know for sure that he was the one who hit me."

Joe reluctantly released his hold on the reporter, and Maguire straightened his rumpled clothes. "For your information, I just got here," he said indignantly. "I didn't hit *anyone* on the head. And I still think you guys and Pierce are making up this whole arson case."

"That's where you're wrong, Maguire," Joe said. "If you don't believe us, call Lieutenant Con Riley of the Bayport Police. He'll back up our story."

The reporter stared at the Hardys for a moment. "Okay, so maybe the fires *were* arson," Maguire said at last. "What does that have to do with me?"

Frank looked Maguire straight in the eye. "Maybe you can tell us," he said. "After all, you covered fires for the D.C. *Chronicle*—before you started trashing that senator in the paper."

Maguire turned pale. "How did you find out about that?" he whispered.

"We asked a very good detective in D.C. to look into your background," Joe said, glancing sideways at his brother.

"You can't pin this on me," said Maguire, becoming flustered. "Maybe I do stretch the facts a little, but only because that's the way Dawson wants it. He's got a real thing about Pierce. The only reason I'm here is because Dawson wants me to do a story on the Buckleys and their neighbors and how they feel about being homeless because of Pierce. I need a good description of the house to add color to my article." He looked angrily at Frank and Joe. "Look, I didn't have anything to do with setting any fires, and I'm not about to lose my job because of your stupid investigation." Maguire turned and stormed off.

Frank stared after Maguire, unconvinced. Maguire was always appearing at crucial moments. Suddenly Frank realized something. He looked down at the ground where he'd been knocked out. "I can't believe it. It's gone!"

"What's gone?" asked Joe.

Frank told him about the partly charred piece of fabric he had found in the well. "Whoever hit me on the head must have taken it," he concluded.

The phone in the van began to ring. Frank ran over, opened the door, and answered it.

"This is Donald Pierce," the voice on the other end of the line said coldly. "I would like to know why I haven't received a report from you yet stating your progress in the arson case."

"We're working on it, Mr. Pierce," replied Frank. "We—"

"That's not good enough," Pierce snapped, cutting Frank off. "I hired you to catch an arsonist, and you have failed!"

Frank tried again. "Mr. Pierce, we—" he began.

"When I hire people, I expect them to do their job," the real-estate developer interrupted. "When they fail, I fire them. You and your brother are fired." With that, he hung up.

Frank hung up the phone and turned to Joe. "He said we weren't doing a good enough job. He's fired us."

"What does he—?" Joe began.

The van's phone rang again, and Frank picked it up. He listened for a few moments, then said, "Sure, Chief," and hung up.

"That was Chief Sullivan. We have to pick up a new fire engine at the factory. But first we need to get the invoice from Scott. Scott was going to pick up the truck, but he was called in to work.

The chief gave me Scott's address," Frank added. "He lives in Heritage Hills."

"I know where that is," Joe said, buckling his seat belt and turning on the ignition. "It's a development of ritzy condos not too far from Kevin's house. You know," he added as he drove down the street, "I'm kind of surprised Scott can afford to live there. Now that I think of it, he has a lot of expensive things, like that new hockey stick and those skates, and that new sports car. He can't make a lot of money working at a supermarket."

"Maybe he saved a lot," Frank said. "Or maybe he has a rich family who helps him out."

When they arrived at the development, Joe parked the van in the space next to Scott's sports car. Then he and Frank headed up the walk to the front door.

When no one answered Joe's knock, he tried the door and found it unlocked.

"I don't think Scott will mind if we just come in," Joe said, pushing the door open. "He probably just stepped outside for a minute."

Joe entered the living room ahead of Frank and glanced around. The room was furnished with expensive-looking chairs, sofas, and tables. On the floor near the TV was a brown garbage bag that looked out of place among the elegant furniture.

"Maybe he's taking out his garbage," Joe said, walking over to the plastic bag. He peered into the bag, then gasped in amazement.

"Frank! Look at this!"

Frank hurried to his brother and looked over his shoulder. The trash bag was piled high with cloth rags.

Then Joe noticed something else. Reaching into the pile of rags, he pulled out a black-and-white ski mask. "The guy I chased last night was wearing a ski mask just like this one," he told Frank.

Just then, Joe heard the front doorknob turn. Joe dropped the ski mask into the trash bag, and he and Frank whirled around just as Scott entered the house. Joe's heart was pounding as he and Frank stepped forward to greet Scott.

Scott was holding a snow shovel and smiling. "I was just helping a neighbor of mine shovel some ice off her walk," he told the Hardys. "I'm glad you guys decided to come in. Hang on a minute and I'll get you the invoice."

"Take your time," Frank said casually.

Scott propped the shovel against the wall and took off his jacket. Then he moved over to a table, picked up a piece of paper, and handed it to Frank. "Here it is."

Frank leaned close to the table as he took the paper. He had noticed a keychain in the shape of a small license plate lying under the invoice. Frank was just able to make out the number: NE 9968.

"Thanks for the invoice, Scott." Turning to Joe, he said, "We'd better get going."

"Have a good time driving that engine," said Scott with a grin as he ushered them out the door. "I always wanted to do that myself. Maybe next time!"

"Scott has to be involved in the arson," Joe said as they pulled out of the Heritage Hills complex. "Those swatches incriminate him. And that ski mask is the one the guy I followed last night was wearing."

"It fits," agreed Frank. He frowned, adding, "He must also be the one who handed me the air pack that was sabotaged."

"I hate to say this, but . . ." Joe began.

"We still need more proof," Frank finished. "What we really need is to catch him in the act. But that might not be so easy, since it means finding out about a fire before it happens."

The factory where Frank and Joe were to pick up the fire engine was part of a large complex on the outskirts of Bayport. When Joe pulled the van up to the gate, he was stopped by a guard, who insisted on checking their invoice.

The guard looked at it, then handed it back to Joe and waved the van through the gate. Joe drove up to a huge building the size of an airplane hanger and got out of the van.

The new fire engine was sitting inside, visible through an overhead door. A large man wearing coveralls came out of the building and walked up to the Hardys. "You here to pick up the engine?" he asked.

Joe showed him the invoice. The man nodded and said, "Well, she's all yours. Bright and shiny and ready for action. Who's going to drive her?"

"No contest," Joe said. Before his brother could make a move, he stepped over to the engine and hoisted himself up into the driver's seat. The man in coveralls handed Joe the keys, and Joe turned on the engine, grinning as it roared to life. "I can't wait to get this baby out on the highway!" he called to Frank. "I want to see how fast she'll go!"

Joe saw his brother roll his eyes and shake his head as he climbed back into the van to follow Joe back to the firehouse.

Despite his excitement, Joe knew it would be foolish to hot-rod in a fire truck. He drove the fire engine very carefully down the highway, staying in the right-hand lane and keeping within the speed limit.

He had only gone a few miles when he saw a vehicle speeding up a curved entrance ramp onto the highway. Joe slowed down a little.

With a shock of surprise, Joe recognized the vehicle. It was the blue van! The van moved onto the highway in front of Joe and picked up speed.

Joe gunned the engine and took off after the van. "You're not getting away this time!" he shouted.

12 A Wild Chase

"Joe, what are you doing?" Frank cried from his van when he saw the fire engine shoot forward. He knew his brother had been kidding when he said he wanted to see how fast the engine would go. Why was he speeding up? Frank accelerated to keep up with him.

Joe concentrated on holding the wheel steady. So far he wasn't having any trouble, and he was still right on the blue van's tail. After all, he realized, the fire engine had been built for speed as well as for carrying fire-fighting equipment.

The blue van turned sharply down an exit ramp, and Joe barely managed to turn the wheel of the fire engine in time to veer onto the ramp after it. He glanced at his rearview mirror and saw that Frank was right behind him. Frank saw the van as it turned onto the ramp, then understood why his brother was driving so fast.

The van zoomed through the yellow light at the end of the exit and continued down a two-lane street. The light turned red just as Joe reached it, but he sped safely through the intersection. A second later he heard the blast of an airhorn behind him and saw in the mirror that Frank had just barely made it past a huge tractor-trailer.

Joe hit the brakes as a car turned onto the two-lane road in front of the fire engine. It moved down the road at a leisurely pace, and Joe watched in frustration as the van pulled farther and farther ahead of him. It was rapidly approaching the end of the road.

I've got to pass this guy, or the van will get away! Joe thought desperately.

He checked to see that the oncoming lane was clear. Joe moved into it and pressed down on the accelerator. He had just passed the slow-moving car when he spotted another car speeding down the oncoming lane toward him. Turning the wheel sharply, Joe swerved back into the right-hand lane just as the oncoming car zoomed past.

Ahead, the blue van reached the end of the road and turned left. Seconds later Joe made the left turn, too. He checked his mirror. Frank had managed to pass the slow-moving car, too, and was still behind him.

They were now driving past a shopping mall that had a parking garage attached. All of a sudden the blue van made a screeching turn into the garage entrance and zoomed up the ramp.

Joe braked the fire engine, pulling it up to the side of the road. There was no way he could maneuver a huge fire truck through the garage. Joe heard a screech of tires as Frank stopped behind him. After jumping off the engine, he ran to the van and got in next to his brother.

"Don't lose it!" Joe cried.

Frank pulled around the fire engine and into the garage. They sped up the winding ramp to the first level, but there was no sign of the blue van. They turned up the ramp again to the second level, and suddenly Joe yelled, "There it is!" The van was parked in front of the stairway that led into the mall.

Frank pulled their black van to a stop, and the Hardys jumped out. They raced over to the blue van. The doors were locked, and the driver was nowhere in sight.

Joe hurried to the stairway and looked around, but he heard Frank say behind him, "Forget it. He's probably hiding somewhere in the mall."

"I guess you're right," Joe said, rejoining Frank by the blue van. Together they began to examine it. "I think it's time to find out exactly what's in here," Joe said. He leaned close to study the single padlock on the double doors at the back of the van. "No problem," he murmured.

Getting a crowbar from his and Frank's van, he began to pull at the lock with all his strength. A minute later the lock popped open and dropped to the floor.

Joe opened the doors, and his blue eyes widened. The back of the van was filled with gas cans, rags, wires, and detonators. A carton of empty beer bottles sat on the floor near the door.

Frank pointed to the carton of beer bottles and said, "That's the same brand as the one that was used to make a firebomb to throw at our garage."

"We'd better call Con and tell him about this." Joe closed the van's doors and replaced the lock. When he was done, he saw that Frank was wiping away the dirt that smudged the blue van's license plate. A moment later he had exposed the letters *NE*. Then the numbers 9968 came into view.

"Joe!" Frank exclaimed, straightening up. "Scott has a license plate keychain with the same numbers on it! I saw it lying on the table under the invoice."

"That just about wraps it up," said Joe. "Scott's our man."

"One of our men," corrected Frank. "I doubt he was working alone." Moving around to the

116

side of the van, he examined it. The paint on the van was peeling, he noticed, and there was a white patch clearly visible underneath. He scratched at the paint, and the white patch grew longer.

"Give me a hand," Frank said to his brother. "I have a feeling something's written under here."

When Frank and Joe had scratched off as much of the paint as they could, they stepped back and gazed at the letters they had revealed.

"'Exam . . .'" Joe read aloud. "And there's a little magnifying glass. That's the logo of the *Examiner!*"

"Right," said Frank. "Which means either Maguire or Dawson is our other arsonist. But which one is it?"

"And who drove the van here?" added Joe. "Maguire, Dawson, or Scott?"

Frank shook his head. "I don't know," he said. "The only thing I'm *pretty* sure about now is that Kevin *isn't* involved."

"I'm really glad to finally hear you say that," Joe said, grinning.

They headed back to their van, and Frank dialed the number of the Bayport Police Department.

"Lieutenant Con Riley, please," he said to the officer at the other end of the line. "This is Frank Hardy."

"Frank?" Con said a moment later. "I'm glad you called. I've got some news for you."

"We have news for you, too," Frank said. "But tell us yours first." Frank hit the speaker button so he and Joe could both hear Con.

"Kevin Thomas was picked up for speeding on the turnpike about an hour ago," Con told them. "The trooper had been alerted about the license and make of Kevin's car, so he took a careful look inside. He found gas cans and a bunch of rags in the well where the spare tire should have been."

"What!" exclaimed Joe. "That's impossible!"

"It's true," said Con. "And one of the rags was a flannel swatch identical to the swatch you found. I'm holding Kevin here for questioning. Now, what's your news?"

Frank told him about the blue van and the explosives and arson materials they had found inside it. He also mentioned his and Joe's theory about both Scott Malone and either Dawson or Maguire working together. There was a short silence over the wire when Frank finished. Then Con said, "I'll send somebody out there for the van right now. Maybe we'll find some prints on it. I'll check out your theory, but I can't rule out Kevin as an accomplice yet. I'll have to hold him here."

After Frank had hung up the phone, Joe turned to him and said, "I think Scott planted that stuff in Kevin's car last night. I mean, we know Scott drives the blue van; he's got the same ski mask I saw the guy wearing; and we found a lot of those swatches in his house."

"Who would ever have thought Scott would do that to his friend," Frank said.

Once the police had arrived to take the blue van, the Hardys drove out of the garage and back to the fire engine. By then it was late afternoon and the sun had already set. Flicking on the headlights of the engine, Joe drove with extra care to the firehouse, with Frank following in the van.

When Frank and Joe finally got home, they found Iola sitting on the sofa in the living room, sipping a mug of hot chocolate.

"Your aunt asked me to stay for dinner," she told them. "She's been keeping it warm on the stove. Where have you guys been, anyway? It's after seven o'clock."

Joe explained what had happened.

"Dawson, an arson suspect!" Iola exclaimed when Joe had finished. "That's really incredible! So I guess Pierce is out of the picture now. That's too bad, because I found something really interesting in his office."

"Tell us anyway," urged Frank. "It might have a bearing on the case."

Iola leaned forward and put her mug on the coffee table. "Well," she began. "I was doing some filing in Pierce's office today when I saw a thick manila envelope marked 'Private.'"

"So naturally you opened it," said Joe.

"Right," Iola replied, grinning. "Inside were several years' worth of Pierce's personal bank statements. They were from banks in New Mexico, Texas, New York City, and Bayport. What was strange about them is that they only showed one deposit a month. And the sums got larger and larger each year."

Frank caught the meaningful look his brother gave him, and he knew they were both thinking the same thing. "Callie told us that Dawson lived in those places, too," said Frank. "It just can't be a coincidence that the two of them keep moving to the same places, especially since they seem to hate each other so much."

"It's almost like one of them is following the other one around just to make trouble for him," Joe put in.

"Wait a minute," Frank said, his eyes lighting up. "Maybe that's just it! What if Pierce has been blackmailing Dawson? That would explain the single deposits getting larger each year. It's common for blackmailers to demand more and more money as time goes on."

Joe nodded. "That also explains why Dawson

hates Pierce so much. Dawson could have planned the fires to get revenge."

The doorbell rang, interrupting their conversation. Frank got up to answer it, checking his watch as he headed for the foyer. It was seven-thirty. Maybe Callie was stopping by to give them more dirt on Dawson, he thought. Opening the door, he peered out into the darkness but saw nothing.

"Is anyone out there?" he called. He heard a rustling noise, but no one came forward. Warning bells sounded in his head, and he quickly reached for the outside light switch.

Just as he flipped it on, a blinding flash ripped through the darkness, and Frank was thrown backward by the force of an explosion.

13 Another Warning

Joe's head snapped around when he heard the blast. He saw Frank hit the wall opposite the door, then fall to the floor. "Frank!" Joe yelled, jumping to his feet and rushing over to him. "Are you all right?"

Frank's eyes were opened, but he looked dazed. "I'm fine," he said slowly. "Check . . . outside."

Joe ran out the door, but whoever had set the explosion was gone. Seeing that the bushes near the door had caught fire, Joe hurried back into the house and headed for the kitchen to get the fire extinguisher.

He rushed past Aunt Gertrude, who had run out of the kitchen to see what was going on. When he came back with the extinguisher a moment later, his aunt was stooped over Frank, a horrified look on her face.

When Joe had doused the flames, he glanced up at the outside light. The fixture had been blown off, ripping a hole in the outside wall above the door. Looking more closely, Joe saw that a thin wire had been attached to the wire that connected the fixture to the inside switch.

Joe stepped back into the house. Iola was kneeling next to Frank on the living room sofa. "Someone set up an explosive device in the light fixture," Joe told them. "It was rigged to go off when the outside light was turned on."

"What kind of creep would do something like that?" Iola demanded angrily. "Your aunt Gertrude could have been the one to turn on that light!"

"The person who set it probably doesn't even know who lives here with us," Frank said. "That explosive device was definitely meant for Joe and me."

"I think dinner would be a good idea," Aunt Gertrude said. The Hardys and Iola headed into the kitchen, where Aunt Gertrude began setting the table.

"Beef stew," Iola said, lifting the lid of a large kettle sitting on the stove. "It smells great!"

She and Joe got three bowls and began ladling out the stew, while Frank used the phone in the kitchen to call Con Riley.

"I want to see if Con can match the explosive device with the ones we found in the blue van," he explained as he dialed the number.

But when he reached the department, the desk sergeant told him that Lieutenant Riley was at a police officers' awards dinner and wouldn't be back until late. Frank asked the sergeant to give Con the message about the explosives if he called in. The officer promised he would and then hung up.

Joe dug into his stew hungrily, polishing it off before his brother and Iola were half done with theirs. "You know," he said, getting up to refill his bowl, "I wonder *why* Pierce has been blackmailing Dawson."

"Oh!" Iola exclaimed suddenly. "I just remembered something. Callie told me she was going to stay late at the *Examiner* tonight to do some snooping around in Dawson's office." She looked at Frank and Joe. "She was kind of nervous about it because he sometimes goes back to the office at night to do work. I tried to talk her out of it, but she insisted. What if Dawson finds her there?"

124

"Why don't we call her and see if she's okay," Frank suggested. "Do you know her number at the office?" he asked Iola.

"Yes. I'll give her a call," Iola said, picking up the receiver and dialing. After waiting a minute Iola drummed her fingers on the tabletop and said, "Hmmm, no answer. I'll try her at home." When Iola again got no response, she looked at Frank and Joe and said, "Now I'm getting worried."

"We'd better go down there to make sure she's not in trouble," Frank said, getting up from the table. "Dawson could have shown up."

As soon as they were all in the van, Frank took off for the *Examiner* office. He parked the van across the street from the office, and he, Joe, and Iola got out and hurried over to the building. As they stepped inside, Frank spotted a uniformed security guard walking into a small room down the hall to their left. He was eating an apple and carrying a copy of the *Examiner*.

"He'll never let us in if Callie isn't answering her phone," Frank said. "We'll have to sneak by him."

Frank, Joe, and Iola tiptoed past the room the guard had entered. Peeking in, they saw he was on the phone, and they took the chance to walk as quickly and quietly as they could into the newsroom. Frank yanked open the doors to the dimly lit room and raced ahead of the others down the aisle toward Dawson's office. When he reached it, Frank saw through the window that the lamp on Dawson's desk was lit.

"I don't see Callie," he said, frowning.

Frank tried the door and found it unlocked. He pushed it open, and the three of them stepped into the office.

"She's definitely not here," Iola said, glancing around the room. "Maybe she didn't find anything and went home already."

Frank was about to pick up Dawson's phone to call Callie's house when Joe called out, "Hey you guys! Come over here. You've got to see what I found!" Frank looked over to see his brother standing by a file cabinet, a manila file opened in his hands.

Joe showed them the file. "This was open on the cabinet. Look inside. There's a letter from a company called Factfinders. It seems Dawson wrote to them asking for information on the statute of limitations on the crime of embezzlement."

"So Dawson wanted to know how long he could be prosecuted for that crime," Frank said when he had finished reading the letter. "And the letter says the statute of limitations passed five years ago."

"But the letter is dated just two weeks ago," Iola pointed out. "And since some of Pierce's bank statements are from Bayport, he's been blackmailing Dawson up until very recently. Dawson must have been furious when he found out he'd paid all that extra money!"

"The fires started not too long after Dawson got this letter," Joe said. "Maybe he set them as double revenge—to get Pierce for blackmailing him *and* for continuing to do it even though the statute of limitations on his crime had run out."

Joe started to put the letter back in the folder. "Hey, there's something else in here," he said suddenly. "A photo."

"It looks like it was cut out of a magazine," Frank said, picking up the photo. " 'Annual Picnic, Horseshoe Bank, Elkhart, New Mexico,' " he read aloud. "And there's Pierce and Dawson standing together smiling with the rest of the staff." He stopped and peered more closely at the photo. Then he looked at Joe and Iola. "There's a bull's-eye drawn on Pierce."

Joe took the photo from Frank. "There's a date written next to Pierce, too. *Today's* date!"

Frank glanced worriedly around the office. "One thing bothers me," he said. "If that file was on the cabinet, Callie must have seen it. I wonder where—"

Just then the phone on top of Dawson's desk began to ring. "That's probably her now." He stepped over to the desk and picked up the phone.

"I've got Callie Shaw," said a man's voice over the line. "Don't come after me and don't call the police, or you'll never see her again!"

14 Kidnapped!

The phone went dead. Frank stared numbly at the receiver for a moment before hanging it up and turning to Joe and Iola. "Dawson's got Callie. He told us not to follow him."

"Oh, no!" exclaimed Iola. "Where do you think he's taking her?"

"My guess is that he's heading for Pierce's," Frank said. "But I don't know if he's going to Pierce's house or his office."

"Let's try calling Pierce's house first," suggested Joe. "That's probably where he is this time of night."

Frank dug into his jacket pocket. "I have the

129

card he gave us on Sunday," he said. He pulled out the card and dialed the home telephone number. After talking briefly with someone on the other end, he hung up again.

"That was the housekeeper," Frank explained to the others. "She said that Pierce is at his office working late."

"His office building is out on Newfield Road," said Iola. "The town council made Pierce build it there because they didn't want a twenty-story high rise in downtown Bayport."

"We're out of here!" Joe said. He, Frank, and Iola burst out of the newsroom, passed the startled guard in a flash, and hurried outside to the van. Joe drove as quickly as he could, following Iola's directions to the outskirts of Bayport.

"Here's Newfield Road," Iola said, and Joe turned down a deserted road bordered on either side by snow-covered fields. "Look, you can see Pierce's building."

Joe had already noticed the huge building that loomed above the glistening snow like a chrome-and-steel monster. It was the only building on the road. As they got closer to it, he could see that all the floors except one were dimly lit by soft night lighting. But the lights in an office on the top floor were blazing brightly. "That must be Pierce's office," Joe said, pointing.

He turned into the entrance and parked the

van in the lot, jumping out a second ahead of Frank and Iola. After racing to the building, Joe plunged through the double doors.

The first thing he saw was a security guard lying on the floor. Joe knelt beside him. "He's out cold. Hit on the head."

Iola ran to the phone on the security guard's desk. "It's dead," she told the others, a frightened look in her eyes.

Joe looked over and saw his brother consulting the directory by the elevator bank. "Pierce's office is on the twentieth floor," Frank said. "Let's get up there!"

Joe jumped to his feet and joined Frank and Iola in one of the elevators. Frank pressed the button for the twentieth floor, and they shot upward.

Suddenly Joe felt the elevator lurch. A second later it bounced to a stop, but the doors remained closed.

Frank pressed the twentieth-floor button again, then tried the lower floors. Nothing happened. He pressed the "Door Open" button, but the doors stayed shut.

"We're only at the fifteenth floor," Joe said, checking the indicator over the elevator doors. "Dawson must have cut the power!" He looked up and saw a small trapdoor set into the ceiling. Pointing to it, he said, "We'll have to climb onto the elevator roof through that door and go up the ladder in the shaft."

"You're right," said Frank, following Joe's gaze. He hoisted his brother up onto his shoulders, huffing from the extra weight as Joe reached for the trapdoor.

Joe grabbed on to the molding around the trapdoor for leverage and gave the door a strong chop with his right hand. It flew open. "Got it!" he exclaimed. He climbed onto the roof and reached down through the opening for Iola.

When she was safely next to him, Joe reached down to help his brother. Frank crouched down a little, swung his hands, and jumped straight up, grabbing on to the edge of the opening. Then Joe hoisted him up, and a moment later Frank, too, was on the elevator roof.

Joe looked around. In the dim light of the shaft, he saw the faint gleam of a metal ladder that ran up the wall. He thought he made out the square shape of an elevator door just above them to the left.

"This way," he told the others, placing a foot on the closest rung and starting to climb. Iola and Frank followed.

They climbed carefully up to the elevator doors, and Joe pressed a button next to the ladder. The double doors to his left instantly slid open. One by one the three of them stepped quickly out of the elevator shaft onto the floor. Without pausing, he raced to the emergency stairs and hurried to the twentieth floor, Frank and Iola right behind him. Once there they paused to catch their breath, peering down the dimly lit hall.

"That must be Pierce's office," whispered Joe, pointing to a bright shaft of light shining out of an office on the left.

The Hardys and Iola stepped slowly and silently down the hall. When they reached Pierce's office, Frank cautiously peered around the corner. There was nobody in the office except Pierce, who was lying on the floor bound and gagged.

Frank hurried into the office, followed by Iola and Joe, and knelt down beside Pierce. Seeing that he was conscious, Frank removed the gag from Pierce's mouth. Joe began to untie the rope around his hands, while Iola worked on the one that bound his ankles.

"What are you doing here?" Pierce sputtered.

"Did you see a girl with Dawson?" Frank asked Pierce.

Pierce shook his head. "All I saw was Dawson. He came in here and grabbed me. After he tied me up and gagged me, he took the key to the office out of my desk drawer and whispered in my ear that"—Pierce hesitated for a moment, shuddering—"that he was going to deliver my final payment." When the ropes were untied, Pierce sat up and began to rub his wrists and ankles.

"Payment for blackmail," said Frank. "That was it, wasn't it? You knew Dawson had embezzled some money from the bank in Elkhart, New Mexico, where you both worked. You promised to keep quiet about it—for a price."

"And you followed him around from place to place to make sure he paid up," added Joe. "Are we right?"

Pierce nodded miserably. "I started my first real-estate company with the money Dawson gave me," he admitted. "But I needed more and more money to build my business, so I kept on blackmailing him."

"Even when you knew the statute of limitations had passed on his crime," stated Frank.

Pierce looked at Frank in surprise. "I didn't know about any statute of limitations," he insisted. "But I figured Dawson had to be the one burning my buildings, setting me up for a fall."

"You couldn't go to the police with your suspicions, though," said Joe. "You were afraid they just might dig too deeply into your past, maybe even check up on those bank statements. That's the real reason you hired us to investigate, isn't it?"

Pierce nodded. "I was worried the police might start thinking that maybe I had burned my own buildings to get the insurance money. They would have checked into my financial situation." He looked at the Hardys. "I figured that a couple of kids like you would do just enough legwork to pin the fires on Kevin—and get the *Examiner* off my back."

"You were also afraid to sue Dawson and the paper for those stories about your negligence," Frank said, "because you were afraid Dawson would tell the police you were a blackmailer."

"That's right," the real-estate developer confessed.

"So Kevin didn't set the fires or cause the warehouse explosion," Frank said, shaking his head.

"But we know who did," added Joe.

"And I'm not *quite* finished yet," a menacing voice suddenly said behind them.

Joe whirled around and saw Sam Dawson and Callie standing in the doorway. Joe could see the fear in Callie's brown eyes. Dawson was holding on to her arm tightly with one hand.

In his other hand was a gun. And it was pointed at Callie's head!

15 A Towering Inferno

"Don't move, any of you," Dawson warned, pulling Callie into the office, "or I'll shoot Callie."

"You!" Pierce exclaimed, staring angrily at the newspaper owner. "I'll get you for setting fire to my buildings!"

"That's only partly true, Mr. Pierce," Frank put in. "Dawson *planned* all the fires, but he had an accomplice to help him set them, a fire fighter." He looked at Dawson. "Didn't you?"

Dawson smiled. "Clever of you to figure that out, Frank. Yes, I had a helper conveniently placed in the firehouse. In fact, here he is now."

Frank saw Scott Malone step into the office behind Dawson and Callie.

"Hi, guys," Scott said, smiling. "Too bad you didn't take our warnings seriously and stop investigating." Scott shook his head sadly. "Somehow, I don't think the hotshot Hardy brothers are going to get out of this one."

"Well, in that case, why don't you tell us how you divided up the work," Frank said. If they could just keep Dawson and Scott talking, Frank thought, he and Joe would have time to come up with a strategy to overpower the two men.

"I set the warehouse fires," Scott said proudly, "with those gasoline-soaked rags."

"Did you throw the canister with the warning note through the window of the warehouse?" Joe asked Scott.

"That was me," Dawson told the Hardys. "After Maguire told me that he had heard you were going to check the warehouse, I figured I'd give you two a little warning. But you continued to interfere with my plan to ruin Donald Pierce!" the newspaper owner cried.

Dawson turned to Pierce. "I've hated you since the day you came to me in Elkhart and first blackmailed me," Dawson snarled at the real-estate developer.

"So you decided to use the power of the press to ruin Pierce's reputation and get him to leave you alone once and for all," Frank said. "And when you found out that the statute of limitations had passed on your embezzlement, you got so angry that you wanted to completely ruin him. So you torched his buildings."

"It was a good plan, you must admit," Dawson said with a chuckle.

While they had been talking, Joe saw that his brother had been moving slightly closer to Dawson. "So who threw the firebomb at our garage?" Joe asked Scott, hoping to keep him distracted. "You?"

Scott nodded. "That's right. And I left you that second warning note, too. But Sam set up the last warehouse explosion and rigged up the device in your light fixture. In fact, that's why I let you guys chase me today. I was giving Sam time to set things up. When I got back to town, I watched you go to the newspaper office, and I let Sam know you were there." He shook his head. "It's too bad I had to leave the van in the parking garage. That was a major mistake."

"It was also a mistake to sabotage my air pack," said Frank.

"And leaving your license-plate keychain on the table," added Joe. "Not to mention the ski mask and flannel swatches in the garbage bag. Why did you do it, Scott?" Joe burst out. "Why did you set up Kevin? He's your best friend!"

138

"I didn't intend to, originally. I got the idea after Maguire overheard Pierce blaming the fires on Kevin at your house last Sunday. I knew framing Kevin would give us the perfect smoke screen. Hey," Scott went on with a shrug, "I *had* to plant those arson materials in his car yesterday. You already suspected him, and I knew the stuff would give you the proof you needed to arrest him. Better him than me."

"And were you the one who hit me on the head at the Buckleys'?" Frank asked, edging even closer to Dawson.

"Sorry about that, Frank," Scott said, "but I had to get that piece of fabric back. And it was me, not Kevin, who hid the warning sign at the pond."

"But how could a fire fighter like you commit a terrible crime like arson?" Iola asked, speaking for the first time.

Scott looked at her, a surprised expression on face. "Are you serious?" he asked in disbelief. "I did it for money, of course." He turned to the Hardys. "How did you think I was able to afford my sports car and all my other great stuff? Not by working as a cashier in a supermarket!"

Joe's hands clenched into fists, and he snarled, "You're a real creep, you know that, Malone?"

"Hey, it was just business," protested Scott.

Dawson offered me a good job with great pay, and I took it."

"That's enough talking," snapped Dawson. "We've got work to do."

Frank was only a few steps from Dawson now. Looking at Callie, he motioned toward the floor with his eyes. A moment later she dived to the floor.

While Scott and Sam momentarily focused on Callie, Frank jumped into action. He lunged toward Dawson and grabbed the hand that was holding the gun.

At the same moment Joe hurled himself at Scott. Scott was the taller of the two, but he was no match for the muscular Hardy brother. Joe grabbed Scott's jacket, then drew his fist back and landed a punch on Scott's chin. Scott staggered back for a moment but then recovered his balance. His face red with anger, Scott charged Joe, but Joe was ready for him. As soon as Scott was close enough, Joe grabbed his arm and twisted it behind his back. Keeping an iron grip on Scott, Joe pushed him to the floor, then looked over to see how Frank was doing.

Frank continued to wrestle with Dawson, trying to get the gun out of the older man's hand. He squeezed Dawson's hand as hard as he could, but the newspaper owner was gripping the gun too tightly. Suddenly Frank doubled over in pain as

Dawson's fist punched him hard in the stomach. He felt his grip loosen and Dawson pull free. When Frank looked up, Dawson was pointing the gun at Joe and Iola.

"Let him up," Dawson ordered. Joe quickly got up off Scott's back.

"Get downstairs and start the engine running," Dawson told Scott. "I'll be down in a minute." Scott nodded and hurried out of the office.

"Now get over there with your brother and Callie," Dawson snapped to Joe and Iola. "Move!"

Dawson stepped back to the doorway. "You made a big mistake blackmailing me all those years, Don," he told Pierce, smiling a little. "I waited a long time to get back at you. And now I'm going to have the best revenge of all."

"Are you going to shoot me?" Pierce whispered.

Dawson shook his head. "Too messy. And I never liked guns anyway. They're just useful for keeping people in line."

Dawson took a deep breath and said, more calmly, "I've got a better way of getting rid of you." He looked at the Hardys and Iola. "Before you got here, Scott and I started a small fire in the electrical system of this building. By now it should be turning into a rather nice-sized blaze."

Pierce stared at Dawson, his face pale. "You're

going to burn down my building?" he asked in disbelief. "But—but you can't do that!" He looked pleadingly at Dawson. "Sam, can't we make some sort of deal?" he pleaded.

Dawson shook his head. "It's too late for deals." He began to back out of the room. Then he stopped and said, "Don't think that the sprinkler system will put out the fire. We've disconnected it. And don't worry about the security guard. He'll be all right. Scott will put him in his car—tied up and gagged, of course." Dawson reached for the doorknob, stepped back into the hall, and pulled the door shut, locking it with a key and leaving the Hardys, Iola, Callie, and Pierce inside.

Frank rushed to the door and tried to open it, but it was locked. He tried the phone, but the line was dead.

"Oh, no! Look!" Callie cried suddenly.

Frank turned and stared up at the ceiling where Callie was pointing. Thick, black smoke was beginning to seep into the room from the ventilation shaft.

Frank looked at the others in horror. "We're trapped!" he exclaimed.

16 Everything's Cool

"We've got to get out of here before this office fills up with smoke," Frank said.

"I'm afraid we need the key to unlock the door," Pierce said.

Frank looked frantically around the office for a way to escape. There was a second door, and he rushed over to it, but it only led to a windowless bathroom. Moving over to the window in the office, he began to feel around it, but stopped when Pierce said, "You can't open any of the windows in this building."

"It would be a sheer drop to the ground

even if we could get out that way," Iola said. "There aren't any ledges on the face of the building."

The smoke was now billowing out of the ventilation shaft, and Frank covered his nose and mouth with one hand. The others had all begun to cough from the dense, stifling smoke.

Then Frank heard a loud click behind him. Turning, he saw that the office door was wide open, and Joe was standing next to it, grinning.

"How did you do that?" Callie asked in an awed tone.

Joe held up a plastic credit card. "I slid it into the space between the door and the frame where the lock is and jiggled it until I was able to push back the bolt."

"How do we get out of the building?" Iola asked in a trembling voice. "We can't use the elevators, and the bottom part of the building is probably in flames."

"We'll have to head up the stairwell to the roof," Frank said. "Maybe somebody has seen the smoke and reported it."

Joe broke into a fit of coughing, then said, "Quick, let's wet some towels or something to help us breathe."

Joe turned to Pierce, who was still sitting in the leather chair, a dazed expression on his face. "Over there," Pierce said, pointing to the bathroom door. "There are some towels and wash-cloths in the cabinet under the sink."

Joe and Iola found five towels and washcloths in the cabinet under the sink and quickly soaked them with water, then handed them to the others.

"Just in time," Callie said, coughing as she pressed her towel to her face.

"We're going to have to crawl out of here and down the hall," Frank told the girls and Pierce. "The smoke isn't so dense near the floor."

The five of them crouched low to the floor and headed down the smoke-filled hall toward the stairwell. When they got there, Joe reached up and felt the door to make sure the fire hadn't reached the stairwell. "It's still cool," he told the others. He pushed the door open, and they all crawled inside and stood up.

Joe led the way up the last flight to the door that led to the roof, followed by Frank, Callie, Iola, and Pierce. Once there, Joe tried the door, but it was locked.

"Stand back, everyone," he ordered. "I'm going to try something."

He took a few steps back, raised his leg, and slammed at the door with the bottom of his foot. The door moved a little but didn't open. Gritting his teeth, he threw his leg out in another tremendous kick. This time the door flew open.

"Nice work," Frank said, smiling at his brother as they all stepped out into the cold, fresh air of the rooftop.

"I know," Joe replied with a grin.

Iola rolled her eyes. "You're so modest," she said to Joe.

"Ah, that's much better," Callie said, breathing deeply. "There's nothing I like better than a smoke-free environment."

"I don't think it's going to stay that way for long," Iola said. She pointed to several two-foot-high, cone-topped vents at the edge of the roof near the door. Thick black smoke was pouring out of them.

"The air will probably spread the smoke around a little," Joe said. "But it's still going to get pretty smoky up here soon. And that means the fire can't be far behind!"

"Now what do we do?" Callie cried, looking at the others helplessly.

Frank noticed that Iola, too, was looking around with increasing panic, while Pierce was still staring numbly into space. Frank tried to think of a way off the roof, but the truth was, he had no idea how they were going to escape.

"Wait a minute!" Frank cocked his head to one side and listened carefully. A faint whirring sound filtered down to them from high above their heads. "Do you hear what I hear?" he asked, looking at his brother.

"It's a police helicopter!" cried Joe, looking up. "And it's heading for the roof!"

Frank was filled with immense relief as the chopper descended slowly and gently touched down on the roof several feet away. Bending low, he started toward it. But when he saw that Pierce hadn't budged and was still staring blankly ahead, Frank helped the man over to the chopper. The others were right behind him. The pilot opened the door on the passenger side and helped Pierce climb in, and Frank and the others climbed in after him.

"This man needs medical attention," Frank told the pilot, indicating Pierce.

"There's an ambulance on the ground," the pilot said. "And a state fire helicopter is on its way to fight the fire from up here." He sped up the rotors, and the chopper lifted up off the roof.

When the chopper landed on the snowy ground near the parking lot a few minutes later, two paramedics came running over with a portable gurney and took charge of Pierce.

After thanking the pilot, Frank, Joe, Callie, and Iola climbed out of the chopper and stood looking at the high rise. Flames had consumed the lower half of the building, and the upper floors were beginning to buckle from lack of support. Despite the steady spray of water coming from several fire engines, Frank knew there was no chance of saving the building.

Shaking his head, he followed the others toward the fire engines. As they approached, Frank saw Con Riley standing next to his car, which was parked near one of the engines. Con turned when he saw them approaching. He was wearing a tuxedo and a topcoat, and Frank recalled that he had been at an awards dinner.

"Am I glad to see you," Con said earnestly.

"How did you know we were here?" Frank asked Con.

"When I got back to the station after the dinner," Con explained, "I got a couple of messages. One was from you asking me to check the explosives in the blue van to see if they matched the device that blew up your light fixture.

"The second message said that you were at Pierce's office building," continued Con, "and that the building was on fire."

Joe gave Con a puzzled look. "But who called in that message?"

"I did," said a voice behind them.

The Hardys turned to see Mark Maguire grinning at them.

Frank stared at the reporter. "How did *you* know we were here?" asked Frank.

"I went back to the *Examiner* tonight to edit some copy," Maguire explained. "The light was on in Dawson's office, and when I went to turn it off, I saw that open file with the letter and photo. I put two and two together and drove over here. I found your van, the security guard tied up in his car, and the building on fire. So I used the phone in your van to call the fire department and the police."

"Thanks," Joe said gratefully to Maguire. "You probably saved our lives."

Frank turned to Con. "Sam Dawson and Scott Malone are the arsonists," he said. "There are five witnesses who heard them confess to setting the fires and causing the explosions. They set this fire, too."

Con nodded. "I'll put out an APB on them right away. They won't get far. And by the way," he added, "I let Kevin Thomas go. We checked the prints on the gas can found in his car. They matched up with Scott Malone's. Oh, I found out why Kevin was late for those fires, too, and why he had to rush away to New York yesterday."

"What was his reason?" asked Joe.

Con smiled. "I think I'll let him tell you."

The next evening the Hardys, Callie, and Iola were sitting at a table in another new pizza restaurant in Bayport.

149

"Does wrapping up a case always make you so hungry?" Callie asked jokingly as Joe reached for his third slice.

"Solving a case and everything else," Frank joked. "Joe will use any excuse to justify his huge appetite."

"Hey, detecting is tough work," Joe said, taking a bite of his pizza. "But seriously, Scott and Dawson are in custody, and Con Riley promised he'd look into Pierce's blackmailing scheme. We deserve to celebrate!"

"Mind if I join you?" a voice above them asked.

Joe looked up and saw Kevin standing by their table, grinning at them.

"Absolutely not," Joe told him, pulling out an extra chair.

"Your aunt told me where you were," Kevin explained as he sat down.

Frank nodded.

"I want to thank you guys for helping to prove I didn't set those fires," Kevin said to the Hardys, "even if you weren't too sure in the beginning."

"Con said he found out why you were late to the fires and why you had to rush off to New York yesterday," said Joe. "Can you tell us?"

Kevin nodded. "I didn't want to tell you before because I was afraid I wouldn't make the grade. I was keeping it to myself, sort of like a good-luck charm. I've been training to become a full-time fire fighter in New York. This morning I got a call from the fire chief in New York."

"And?" Frank said, leaning toward Kevin.

"And I've been hired by the department to be a New York City fire fighter," Kevin replied, his face shining.

Joe clapped his friend on the back. "Now that," he said with a grin, "is *really* hot news!"

THE HARDY BOYS® SERIES By Franklin W. Dixon